What the critics are saying

"We travel through worlds and cultures, seeing bizarre customs (always related to sex or gender behavior) in each new village. No Mercy was a great story, and a wonderful expansion into the Trek Mi Q'an universe. The sex is hot. Very hot, though there is a plot (and a good one) wending through the story. Again, Jaid Black at her finest." - *Ann Leveille for The Best Reviews*

"*No Mercy* is the decidedly wicked sequel to *The Empress' New Clothes*. The quick pace filled with an abundance of sex is enhanced by the moments of humor. Fans of erotic romance will enjoy this sexy adventure into the seventh dimension...You won't want to miss *No Mercy*." - *Terry Figueroa, Romance Reviews Today*

"There is no end to the excitement, sexually and adventure wise. Oh, baby! Don't miss out on all the fun. Get reading!" - *reviewer Suzanne Coleburn*

Trek Mi Q'an Series

Ellora's Cave Publishing, Inc.
PO Box 787
Hudson, OH 44236-0787

ISBN # 0-9724377-4-6

Edited by Cris Brashear.
Cover art by Bryan Keller.

Warning: The following material contains strong sexual content meant for mature readers. *No Mercy* has been rated NC-17, erotic, by three independent reviewers. We strongly suggest storing this book in a place where young readers not meant to view it are unlikely to happen upon it. That said, enjoy...

NO MERCY

A Trek Mi Q'an Tale

Written by

Jaid Black

WARNING:

No Mercy is part of a series and not meant to stand alone. We suggest reading *The Empress' New Clothes* by Jaid Black before attempting to read this novel.

To Giselle McKenzie, a new and hilarious friend
— this hero's for you ;)

"A pain stabbed my heart as it did every time I saw a girl I loved who was going the opposite direction in this too-big world." - *Jack Kerouac*

Prologue

Blood and broken bodies dotted the landscape of the blue crystal battlefield, hoards of defeated insurrectionists gasping what would be their last breaths on this side of the Rah. He stood like a vengeful golden god amongst the carnage of the slain, fangs baring from his gum line as a blood-curdling growl erupted from the depths of his throat. The colors of his eyes quickly shifted back and forth — blue to green, green to blue, and back again — like crazed pulses of energy that could not be turned off.

Kil, the king of Morak, stilled, his glowing blue eyes widening as he watched the metabolic changes overtake his younger brother.

Time was running out for Rem, he thought with heavy hearts.

The madness had already come upon him.

Chapter 1

The Ice Palace On The Moon of Sypar
Stronghold of Planet Tryston
Trek Mi Q'an Galaxy, Seventh Dimension
6040 Y.Y. (Yessat Years)

Rem Q'an Tal, King of Sypar, High Lord of the Gryok Sectors, and master of all he surveyed, rested his head upon the lush naked breasts of Yoli, the favored of his bound servants. Lying upon his royal high-bed, Rem's glowing blue eyes flicked dispassionately about, taking in everything, missing nothing, whilst she massaged all tension from his shoulders.

Even as Yoli administered to his shoulders, the nipples from her plump breasts jabbing seductively into his back, another naked bound servant sat on her knees beside his reclining form, her hands rubbing about his heavily-muscled torso, her breasts within tongue distance that she might offer him a nipple to suckle of should he desire it.

A third naked bound servant, and the lustiest suckler His Majesty owned, paid homage to his manhood, her lips and throat devouring the length of his ever-erect shaft. A fourth bound servant administered to his man sac, her eyes closed in bliss as his scrotum began to tighten in her mouth.

The fifth and final bound servant lay at Rem's feet, her clit rubbing against the toes of one foot, her lips and tongue sucking the toes of the other. She convulsed repeatedly against the foot her clit rubbed, saturating the king with her woman's dew.

Rem spoke not a word as the wenches he had acquired in war saw to his needs. 'Twas his right as their master to take from them what he would, to delight in the feel of so many lips and lusty tongues running up and down the length of him. Though none of these wenches were slaves to him as his two hundred female *Kefas* were, they were all bound to him for varying lengths of time—all of them prisoners of war, all of them accepting their lots in life as no more than the king's sexual chattel.

Closing his eyes and turning his face toward the plump breasts of the bound servant massaging his chest, Rem's tongue curled around one of her proffered nipples, drawing it into the warmth of his mouth and sipping from it. She shuddered, running long fingernails through his silky golden hair as she pressed his face in closer to her chest. Her fingernails found the three braids plaited at either temple, then brushed beneath them to comb through the mass of golden hair that fell below his shoulders.

The bound servants attending to Rem's cock and man sac grew lustier, both of the wenches suckling him frenziedly. He groaned against the nipple his mouth was latched onto, luxuriating in the feel of so much female flesh catering to his every whim.

Or luxuriating as much as was possible.

For seventeen Yessat years, ever since the High Queen and Empress Kyra Q'ana Tal had snatched his bridal necklace from the severed head of the cunning Jera, Rem had searched the galaxies in an effort to find his true Sacred Mate. He had searched in six dimensions and more star systems than he cared to recall. But alas, it always came back to this...

Rem's body convulsed as he spurted into the greedy mouth of Lytch, the bound servant attending to his shaft. He sighed when it was done, wondering to himself how it was possible to spew for these wenches when he'd never felt such a lack of arousal in all of his days.

Mayhap the average warrior on Tryston, a humanoid male unable to afford the multitude of bound servants and slaves Rem owned, would find such a scenario enticing. And mayhap he would have too, were it not for the fact that his sire had given him his first harem at thirteen Yessat years. For what amounted to hundreds of years in the primitive time-keeping dimensions, Rem's every moon-rising had been the same. He was jaded. Hopelessly jaded.

"Your Majesty," a feminine voice called out from across the bedchamber, "You've visitors to see you."

Rem's icy blue eyes flicked towards the voice. It belonged to Muri, a bound servant owing him but one more Yessat year's worth of servitude. Topless, her breasts bobbing up and down as she walked towards the royal high-bed, she wore no clothing save the transparent *qi'ka* skirt all wenches of Tryston donned.

"Come forward and deliver your message, Muri." Rem's dark, shadowed voice rumbled low throughout the bedchamber. His brooding gaze fell to the thatch of dark black curls at her mons, easily seen through a *qi'ka* so transparent. He idly wondered if she would be able to bring him to a higher peak than the blonde wenches still attending to his cock and man sac had. "And remove your *qi'ka* whilst speaking."

Muri bowed low, her nipples hardening at the king's words. She shuddered with delight, knowing he meant to impale her the soonest. Standing up from her bow, she was careful to keep her gaze submissively lowered whilst she shed her transparent skirt and delivered the message to the king. "'Tis Lord Death and your brother King Kil to see you, Your Majesty. Shall I announce them?"

Rem nodded once, his glowing eyes raking over her naked mons and her lovely tanned skin. "Aye. Send them in before attending to me."

Muri bowed again, then scurried towards the bedchamber doors. Less than a Nuba-minute later Rem watched his good friend Death and his only non-mated brother Kil stride into his rooms. He paid no attention to Muri who even now was climbing atop his muscled body and impaling herself on his shaft with a moan.

One corner of Rem's mouth kicked up into a semi-grin as the two warlord giants strolled towards the raised bed. "'Tis good to see you brother, and you as well Death, my friend."

Death grunted, the ominous skull tattooed across his forehead crinkling slightly, indicating that the eight-foot mammoth was well-humored. He threw a flat bottle of *matpow* at Rem who caught it easily during its mid-air flight. "'Tis moonshine from my sector," he grumbled.

Kil's lips kicked up into a semi-grin reminiscent of Rem's. It was ironic indeed that two natural brothers so alike in temperament were polar opposites in looks. Where Rem was fair-haired like their brother King Dak, Kil's dark hair favored their eldest brother, the Emperor Zor.

All brothers, however, possessed the glowing blue orbs of the Q'an Tal bloodline as well as the richly tanned skins inherited from their sire. And all brothers possessed the Q'an Tal height, surpassing seven and a half feet or better.

It was only Rem and Kil, however, who had reputations amongst the Q'an Tal brothers as ruthless, merciless warlords. Where Dak and Zor were easily humored and quick to jest, Rem and Kil were not. Of course, the other two Q'an Tal brothers had reasons to be cheerful. Both had acquired their Sacred Mates nigh unto eighteen Yessat years prior and both had become sires multiple times since the claimings.

Kil nodded once. "'Tis sweet bliss for a certainty, Death's moonshine."

Rem took a deep swallow of the *matpow*, his throat muscles bobbing up and down as he did so. Finishing the flask's contents, he sighed lustily, the moonshine having had a more pleasing effect on him than the wenches rubbing and kissing upon his body, even better that the effect of the wench riding him hard. "I hope you've brought more for our quest into the first dimension." He absently reached up and toyed with Muri's nipples, paying her no more heed.

Death grunted, a sound Rem had come to learn meant "aye".

"Speaking of the quest, I've some bad news," Kil informed his reclining brother. His gaze flicked over the naked wenches attending to him.

Rem quirked one golden eyebrow in response.

"I cannot join you two this go-round." Kil sighed, running a large hand through his black mane of hair. "Signs of new insurrectionist activity have cropped up in the far sectors."

"They've acquired a new leader?"

"Aye. Tibo I've heard him called."

Rem studied his brother's harsh features. If insurrectionists were involved, there would be no dissuading Kil from waiting to see to the battling until they'd returned from the first dimension. This he knew. Their mother, after all, had been raped and murdered at insurrectionist hands, Kil having been forced as a man-child to watch as the black deed had been done. "I see." He waved a hand toward him. "Then I will join you in the battling, brother. I can resume my hopeless search upon the capture of the—"

"Nay!" Kil bellowed, unable to contain his fierce reaction. He glanced toward Death, noting that the giant appeared worried as well—sweat had broken out on the skull across his forehead. Flicking his gaze back towards Rem, he forcibly gentled his voice. "I think it best do you search for your *nee'ka* without me this time, brother. If you are unsuccessful I will accompany you on the next quest."

Rem's eyes narrowed into glowing blue slits. "You have been as long without a Sacred Mate as have I, indeed, a few Yessat years longer. Why should I resume questing about the galaxies and leave the blood-work to you?"

Because you frighten me, Kil thought to himself. "Because this is my battle. And because 'tis my desire to walk alone. I need not your help to flush them out, brother."

Kil's eyes bore into Rem's. He wanted not for the King of Sypar to question him further. He wanted for his brother to find his mate. And quickly. Before time ran out. Before Rem began devolving, before the metabolical changes began to accelerate and he was forever damned to becoming a—

Nay! Kil thought fiercely. Not Rem. Not the brother he had always been so close to. He could not allow it.

Were Rem any other warrior, a warrior who had not been forced to endure year after year after year of a bleak existence with no hope for redemption, then perhaps he would be faring better than he was. But such was not the case. The years with Jera had made Rem harsh, merciless. The years after Jera's death, unable to locate his Sacred Mate, had squelched his barely kindled sense of hope all the further, creating a man so grim and frightening that even he, Kil Q'an Tal, the king of the ever-feared red moon Morak, shuddered at the thought of what would happen if—

Nay...he would not think of it.

"Go, brother," Kil said firmly, his tone broaching no argument. "You forget that Death has the need of heirs as well. 'Tis not recommended for any warrior to quest about without aide into star systems unknown to our people." His ice-blue gaze so much like Rem's flicked over the form of the eight-foot tall giant. His mouth tilted slightly upwards in a wry grin. "Though primitive men would have to be as daft as a Yessat day is long to mess with our friend here."

Death merely grunted.

Rem discarded the latter part of his brother's statement as irrelevant, latching onto the important piece of what he'd just said. Death *was* in need of heirs as much as he himself was in need of them. He nodded, convinced. "Aye, 'tis true." He looked to Kil. "And since I know you to be a proficient hunter I will do your bidding...*this once.*"

Death appeared pleased by such news. "I go to prepare the gastrolight cruiser for our departure. 'Twill be ready the soonest."

Indeed, Kil thought, the giant must be extremely pleased to have spoken such a long sentence in the first. It was only when Lord Death was feeling particularly pleased that he deigned to speak in more than one or two word phrases. Well, that and when he thought to woo a wench to the *vesha* hides. Leastways, Death had been quite the talker two moon-risings ago on Morak whilst sampling of the fair Typpa's charms. "I shall go with him anon to see the deed done."

Rem waved Kil away. "I offer you the use of my *Kefas* and bound servants to see to your needs when I've departed, brother." He kneaded Muri's buttocks, her woman's channel still trying to milk him for life-force even after she'd ridden him into her woman's joy four times. "Muri and Lytch are gifted of tight, wet channels should you desire to rut in them."

Kil's glowing blue eyes flicked over the wenches in question. "Aye. Have them bathed and sent to my rooms the soonest. In fact, send a few more along with three or four of your most talented *Kefas*. I've the need to work out my lust."

"'Tis done."

Kil inclined his head to his brother then followed Death from the royal bedchamber. Before he telekinetically summoned the doors shut, he stole one last glance at Rem's reclining form, watching as he convulsed into Muri's channel.

He was changing. Kil had noticed it for the first time three Yessat years past whilst warring together in a sector on Tron plagued with insurrectionists. The years had taken their toll, the grimness of Rem's countenance a constant.

During the following three years the signs of his brother's change had worsened in their intensity, Rem having had near-delirious bouts of madness overcome him on a few occasions. It was so bad on the last of these occasions that the Q'an Tal men took Rem to the Chief Priestess Ari for spiritual and sexual healing. He had rutted in the beautiful Chief Priestess' channel for nigh unto a straight fortnight before feeling well enough to seek his own palace.

And the signs continued to grow worse, to become more fully developed. Death had informed Kil that not even a full sennight ago Rem had lost control of himself whilst arguing with a visiting lesser king. The lesser king had nearly died, had almost been telekinetically suffocated to death by a low-growling, nearly crazed Rem.

'Twas the growling that made Kil uneasy for it was the most recognizable of all the signs and the one closest in proximity to the inevitable metabolic changes that would slowly metamorphosis Rem into another, baser self.

Devolution. Every unmated warrior's fear; every unmated warrior's potential reality.

Kil thumped Death on the back, wishing him well. "I bid peace and prosperity unto you, my friend."

"And I unto you."

Kil hesitated before taking the twisting ice-jewel staircase that would see him to his rooms. "Please have a care for Rem. I ask that you keep him from all situations that might cause him to—"

"'Tis done." Death inclined his head, knowing the king's thoughts for they were already his own.

Kil met his gaze. "Summon the Chief Priestess if need be. Ari is the only amongst us powerful enough to give aide should he begin to...devolve."

At Death's grunt Kil nodded once, then disappeared up the winding staircase to have his comforts seen to.

Chapter 2
Shoreham, Australia
Present Day Earth

Giselle McKenzie's mouth pinched together in a tight-lipped frown as she regarded her dinner date from across the slight expanse of the small, intimate table for two in the restaurant where they were seated. Had it come to this? she thought grimly. Had she truly become so desperate for male company that she was willing to give away her virginity to this hog in men's clothing?

Giselle's nostrils flared wickedly as she watched Anthony slurp up another helping of spaghetti from his plate, sauce clinging to his chin as he attacked his entree. The scene playing out before her brought to mind a pig dining at his trough, except for the fact that pigs usually don't make such a horrid mess of themselves.

She sighed, her expression remote as she set her elbow atop the table and plopped her chin down onto the palm of her hand while she watched him eat. "Are you enjoying your meal?" she asked blandly.

"Tremendously," Anthony intoned through bites of the sticky red pasta.

Giselle winced, the sight of the half-eaten spaghetti strands showing between his teeth more than she could stomach looking at. She briefly closed her eyes, then took a steadying breath and straightened up in her seat.

No matter how bad Anthony's table manners, she told herself firmly, she *would* see this evening through. After tonight she would no longer be a virgin. After tonight she wouldn't have to carry around the secret shame that came with the knowledge that she'd never known a man's bed...and she was thirty-six years old.

Where had the years gone? she asked herself nostalgically, the state of her maidenhood still somewhat surreal-seeming to her. It wasn't that she was a prude or undesirous of male company — that was most definitely not the case. It's just that the opportunity for a relationship with a man had never presented itself at her country doorstep. And she had never gone out of her way to remedy the situation — until now.

But now, after thirty-six years of spinsterhood, of having never known a man's touch, she was determined to change the course of her existence. And she was determined that it would change tonight.

Giselle had spent her early twenties as a shy and withdrawn girl. She had preferred perfecting her equestrian skills over worrying about snagging dates with members of the opposite gender. By the time she'd finally overcome her shyness in her late twenties she hadn't had any time to commence an active social life then either for her father, at the time her sole surviving parent, had become ill with a rare blood disease and had needed her constant attendance. As is the case for most people world-round, their family hadn't had enough money to hire a professional nurse, so the job had been Giselle's from the first — not that she had minded.

But her father, the only person in the world she had ever truly loved, had lingered amidst his illness for seven long years. She had cherished each and every moment she'd had with him and had done everything in her power to make his painful existence as comfortable as possible.

There had been times when it had been difficult, times when she had sat up crying at night because she knew that no matter what she did the end result would inevitably be the same. And, indeed, it had been. He had died almost seven years to the date of his original diagnosis and had left Giselle empty, broken, and utterly alone.

She had grieved for the loss of her father for a little over a year. And now, at the age of thirty-six, she realized that life had somehow managed to pass her by and that it was time to reclaim some of the youth she'd lost.

Giselle was a woman of average looks, neither hopelessly plain nor heart-stoppingly beautiful. At five feet four inches in height, with a long straight mop of strawberry-blonde hair, and pale skin with a splash of freckles here and there, she didn't feel that there was anything all that remarkable or recommendable about her looks. She wasn't a dark-haired exotic, nor a tanned, blonde Barbie doll, nor a red-headed vixen. She was just Giselle McKenzie, an average woman of average appearance.

If there was anything particularly fetching about her, she conceded, it was her large, green eyes. Somehow, amidst her ivory skin and the freckles dusted here and there, they managed to sparkle, to make a rather ordinary face seem a bit more appealing. A bit. But probably not by much.

Giselle, however, was not the type of woman to waste her time wishing she was somebody else or wishing that she would become a miraculous beauty overnight. She would work with what she had and hope it was enough. And Anthony's interest in her had proved that it was enough for at least him. Not that he himself was anything to write home about, she thought morosely.

Bloody hell! Would the man never stop drooling that ghastly spaghetti sauce?

Her chin going up a notch, Giselle relegated all misgivings concerning what she was about to do tonight to the back of her mind. She *would* see this through. She *would* go to Anthony's bed. She *would* — finally! — be rid of her unwelcomed and unwanted hymen. And then she would be able to resume her country life without feeling so wretchedly inadequate.

Whatever happened between her and Anthony after this night, or her and any other man for that matter, was up to fate. She was determined not to worry about it, to let life happen as it were. But, she thought with a sense of inward satisfaction, at least she would be letting fate take its course sans her maidenhead. A bloody embarrassment, that.

"So tell me more about yourself," Giselle said, refusing to look anywhere below Anthony's eyes lest the sight of his eating make her ill. "How long have you been the manager of the grocery store in town?"

Anthony spoke through mouthfuls of pasta. "About eleven years now."

"I see. And do you like it?"

"Yeah."

She tapped her nails on the tabletop, considering what else could be said. "What do you like to do for fun?" she asked conversationally.

"Play cards."

"Do you win much?"

"Yeah."

Giselle sighed. This was definitely the most boring conversation she'd ever had the displeasure of partaking in. It only irritated her all the more that her date for the evening, the first one she'd had in more years than she cared to contemplate, was more interested in his meal than in her. She remembered her maidenhead and plowed on determinedly. "Which card game is your favorite?"

"Poker." This with three large spaghetti strands dangling from his chin.

Her lips tightened. "That sounds rather interesting. Perhaps you could teach me how to play."

"Maybe."

Bloody hell! Couldn't the man say more than one word at a time!

"Would you like to have sex with me?"

The sound of Anthony's fork clanging against his plate at least brought Giselle a feminine sense of satisfaction in knowing that she had well and truly rattled the damned man. She smiled like a woman of the world feeling terrifically smug for a thirty-six-year-old virgin.

"Wh-What?" he squeaked out. Tugging at his tie, Anthony considered her through bulging eyes.

"I said would you care to have sexual intercourse with me this evening?" She thought of her hymen and immediately decided she was taking no chances he'd not heard her correctly. "You know," she said magnimoniously, waving a hand about, "have sex, make love, do the dirty deed."

Her eyes narrowed as she looked at his shocked expression, wishing that any man but this pasta-inhaling wimp would be the one who would take her virginity. The course, however, had been set. Besides, she thought bitterly, she'd just purchased two damned cats last week. Enough was enough. "Be a man," she seethed through clenched teeth. "Take me to bed."

Anthony gulped, his Adam's apple bobbing up and down. "Okay," he squeaked.

Giselle sat up straighter in her chair, the feel of victory surging through her veins. She felt as though she'd just won the Olympic gold, climbed the highest mountain, swum the deepest of oceans. That her major accomplishment was getting the moron across from her to agree to sever her hymen wasn't of consequence.

What was important, she told herself staunchly, was that within the next few hours she would know the delights of being with a man. Or, she thought with down-turned lips, she would at least know what it was to be with a man. She doubted much in the way of delight would factor into the equation.

That last thought caused her determination to falter a bit, but when she reflected back on her recent feline purchases she regained her rigid stance. She was so preoccupied with her thoughts that she failed to realize the bracelet that was dangling from her wrist had managed to unclasp itself and fall to the ground. "Shall we leave then?"

Anthony's jaw went slack. "W-Well..." — he cleared his throat — "where shall we..." — his face colored as he lowered his voice — "have sexual intercourse at?" he whispered.

Bloody hell! Must she think of everything!

Giselle's nostrils flared. "In the car, at your flat, at my house. I don't particularly care. Let's just get the show on the road so to speak."

Anthony gawked at her a moment or two before regaining his senses. He'd never had a woman throw herself at him quite so brazenly. His erection was stone-hard. "W-Well..." — he reached across the table and placed his hand atop hers as his voice went down in timbre — "the car will do fine I — *ouch!*" He snatched his hand back with a howl.

Giselle shook her head, not understanding. She heard a low growl resonating in the back of her mind but, thinking it no big deal, discarded it as irrelevant. Someone must have brought a seeing-eye dog into the restaurant or something. "What is it? What's wrong?"

"You stabbed me with the fork!" he whined.

She took offense at that. "I most certainly did not."

"Then why am I bleeding?"

Giselle's gaze fell to his bloodied hand to quickly ascertain that, indeed, the hammy thing truly was bleeding. "I've no notion," she said in a bewildered voice. "I wasn't even holding my fork." She had brushed against it with her pinky finger, but hadn't realized it.

Anthony looked at her speculatively for a protracted moment, then decided she must be telling the truth. The woman had invited him to her bed, or in this case, her car. Why would she stab him before getting a piece of him? He smiled. "Of course you aren't responsible, darling," he crooned.

Darling? she thought.

"It was obviously no more than a bizarre accident." He reached across the tabletop and laid his hand atop hers once again. "Shall we—*ouch!*"

Giselle watched in shock and horror as the fork that had been laying under her hand on the tabletop catapulted from its resting place and hurled itself straight toward Anthony's eye. He turned his head at the last possible moment and the four-pronged eating utensil lodged itself in his cheek instead. She screamed.

The low growling sound grew wilder, frenzied, crazed-sounding. She covered her ears, her mouth hanging open dumbly as she gawked at Anthony and tried to figure out what was happening. Her heart-rate was inexplicably high. She was sweating bucket-loads even though the restaurant was kept at a cooled temperature. Feelings of primordial anger and possessiveness swamped her. But they weren't her own feelings. They were somebody else's. A man's. A male who meant to punish her if she didn't...

"I'm hurt!" Anthony wailed. "I need a doctor!"

Giselle broke out of her trance and shot to her feet, discarding all of the weirdness of the situation as irrelevant and focusing on the tangible. "I'll drive you to the hospital," she said breathlessly, the strangest feeling of fatigue overpowering her. It took her a long moment to snap out of it. "L-Let's go."

* * * * *

"Control yourself, my friend." Death braced his hands on either of Rem's shoulders to steady him. He swallowed roughly as Rem cocked his head and, teeth bared and growling, regarded him with murder in his eyes. The king's eyes, he noted worriedly, were shifting back and forth from blue to wild green, as if an electrical current was running into his head and repeatedly flicking the colors back and forth.

He had to stop him from changing, had to bring a halt to any further devolution. By the sands, Death thought grimly, let this not happen now when we have finally found his wee bride! "We will take your *nee'ka* when darkness falls, my friend. *Now snap out of it anon,*" he barked.

Death was relieved that the rough edge to his voice produced the desired effect and the king's eyes began to shift back to blue. A glowing green pulsed through them once more, then flicked off completely and resumed their natural hue. He took a breath of relief.

"I do not want," Rem ground out, "to wait until the moon-rising to claim her." His muscles corded and tensed as he watched his Sacred Mate scurry into some sort of metal box with the man who had dared to touch her. A moment later a primitive engine contraption roared to life and the metal box fled the parking facility altogether.

He wanted the primitive man dead. Annihilated from existence. His teeth slowly began to bare...

"'Tis best do we shield the primitives from the claiming," Death grumbled, meeting the king's eyes. "You've a lock on her scent. 'Tis impossible for the wee wench to flee."

Rem ran a large hand over his jaw line and took a deep breath. He knew that changes had begun to take place within him. He could feel his mind cracking and slipping. He needed that wee wench and he needed her now. Being forced apart from her was sheer torture. Even waiting until nightfall felt like an eternity.

But he was a king. And because of that fact he knew the way of their people better than most. 'Twas unnecessary and mayhap disastrous to alert any primitives to the existence of other humanoids. They would find out in their own time as they plotted out the course of their own destinies.

Rem took a deep breath, calming the rate of his hearts simultaneously. His blue eyes flicked a warning green once, and then, with the force of sheer will-power, he tamped down his predatory nature and saw once more through sane eyes. "We will wait..." he rumbled out, his gaze flicking toward the metal box that was making a turn and heading down some manner of paved street. He fingered the bridal necklace he was clutching. "Until darkness falls."

Chapter 3

What a day! Giselle thought dramatically as she fell onto her bed with a groan. Placing a cool cloth over her eyes, she gloomily considered what had become of her intricately formulated plans.

They had been reduced to rubbish. All of them.

Her date had been a tiring bore, he had inexplicably been stabbed in the cheek with a fork, she had rushed him to the local hospital whereupon he had garnered five stitches for his trouble, and as if all that were not bad enough, she thought with a snarl, he had refused to allow her to pull off to the side of the road so he could quickly deflower her before carrying on to the hospital. The wimp.

Bloody hell! What wretched luck I have!

The sound of cats meowing in the background made Giselle's tight-lipped expression that much stiffer. What in the blazes had ever possessed her to purchase two cats was beyond comprehension. She might as well paint the word "pathetic" across her forehead in glowing neon pink and be done with it.

Well, she sniffed, at least she could take comfort in the love of her ever-faithful pet poodles, Bryony and Tess. They had been her beloved companions for over three years, giving her soft, sweet fur to cry into as her father's condition had worsened. And better yet, owning poodles was in no way associated with spinsterhood. She'd have to give the damn cats away to Mrs. Hiram three miles down.

Bryony and Tess jumped up onto the bed moments later, whining about something or another. She wrapped an arm around both of them, comforting them with her scent and touch. The dogs were nervous, she absently noted as she petted both of their fluffy sides. About what she couldn't begin to imagine. It wasn't as if anything exciting ever happened in dull Shoreham. Indeed, she seethed, women couldn't even seem to lose their virginity in this damned hole of a town.

Giselle harrumphed, deciding that whatever had the girls spooked was liable to go away. Perhaps a rodent had scurried by outdoors or something. Whatever it was it would go away if it knew what was in its best interest. She was, after all, in no mood to be bothered.

Giselle's eyebrows shot up from below the damp cloth when it dawned on her that her nightgown was coming undone. Not just undone, she thought in shock, but it was also being...*ripped to shreds?*

Tearing the cloth off of her face, her eyes shot open and clashed with a glowing blue gaze. She could not move, could not speak, felt helplessly paralyzed as the man's form drew nearer to the bed and moonlight revealed a giant so huge that she damn near fainted.

The man's eerie gaze held her steady, immobilized. Sweat broke out onto her forehead as her nipples stabbed upwards and puckered from the chill in the air. The giant seemed to notice her body's reaction for he reached out and plucked a hardened nipple between his overly large fingers, then rolled it around as he continued to stare into her eyes.

Giselle gasped, in so much shock she began to feel hysterical. That condition, coupled with the bizarre paralysis she was feeling, caused her to go numb. She tried to look away from him, tried desperately to reclaim her body, but she couldn't. It was as if that man, that...giant...held all dominion over her.

His hand released her nipple and he sat down on the edge of the bed beside her. Those bizarre blue eyes hungrily raked over her as the fingers of one hand splayed through the thatch of strawberry-blonde curls between her thighs. She gasped again, her breathing growing labored.

She couldn't see much of the man, could just make out his exceedingly tall and thickly muscled form. And the piercing blue eyes. God in heaven, she thought hysterically, what kind of man possessed eyes like that?

Giselle began panting as the giant's hands came toward her neck wielding some sort of a bizarre necklace that pulsed in vibrant colors no words could describe. Did he mean to strangle her with it? she thought hysterically. Would he kill her right here in her own bed?

Unable to endure the suspense, her eyes rolled back into her head as she slowly swooned into oblivion. Her last thought was that after she'd come so close to having sex with Anthony tonight, she was about to die a virgin. Or worse yet, die a non-virgin who'd been raped by Paul Bunyon.

Bloody hell! What a wretched day!

* * * * *

After barking at Death to make haste to the gastrolight cruiser with his *nee'ka's* yipping animal friends, Rem picked up the naked body of his sleeping wee wife and hoisted her up into his arms.

He smiled. Actually smiled. 'Twas the first time he'd done so in more Yessat years than he cared to contemplate.

'Twas done. And she was his.

After years of searching the galaxies only to be defeated at every turn, he had at last acquired the only woman in existence biologically capable of completing him. He tightly held onto her naked body as a current of gastrolight beamed the King and Queen of Sypar up into the belly of the ship which hovered on the far side of the moon, safely undetected by the primitives.

'Twould take but a few moon-risings to reach Tryston and present his *pani* bride to his family. And then, he thought with a predator's satisfaction, 'twas but a mere consummation feast that stood betwixt their joining.

Rem bent his neck to sweetly kiss the tip of her nose. 'Twas spotted, he noted in awe, spotted just as the images of the goddess Aparna were spotted. His shaft so erect it was broaching pain, Rem walked faster toward their bedchamber aboard the cruiser, eager to examine his new prize.

When he reached their rooms he laid her out carefully upon the bed, then hoisted himself up beside her. Summoning off his warrior's garb, he sat on his knees next to her and ran his trembling hands all over her. Her hair, her face, her breasts and nipples, the soft thatch of hair between her thighs...it was all his.

By the goddess, he thought reverently, his wee *pani* bride had been worth the hellish years of waiting. Never had he beheld a woman more beautiful. 'Twas fact that his elder brothers had mated with women possessed of rare skins, one an onyx and the other, like Rem's *nee'ka*, with the coloring of a *sekta* pearl. But neither of his brothers could boast of having claimed a *sekta* pearl wench with spots.

"Just like the goddess," he murmured, still in awe of his good fortune. A dusting of light spots across her face and another slightly darker smattering on the swell of her bosom brought to mind the sweet confection of *migi*-candies. He felt his mouth drying out even as he offered up a quick prayer of thanks to Aparna.

Rem reclined down beside his *nee'ka's* slumbering form and reverently ran his hands all over her body. Her nipples stabbed upwards in reaction and with a groan he bent his neck and sipped one into his mouth.

Her breasts were small, he noted, but her nipples were thick and long, bedeviling in their beauty. Truth be told, Rem couldn't have cared one way or the other how large or small her breasts were. Leastways, he conceded with a grin, they would be filled with sweet juice the soonest.

Closing his eyes, his dark eyelashes fanned downward as he contentedly drew from his *nee'ka's* nipple. He fell asleep clutching her tiny form close to him, his lips attached to the rosy peak as if they were a part of it.

Chapter 4

"Who," Giselle said distinctly, each word enunciated through set teeth, "are you?" She could only gawk at the profile of the blonde-haired giant who reclined next to her, his fingers playing connect-the-dots with the freckles splashed across her bosom. "And what are you doing?"

Bloody hell! She'd been kidnapped by a pervert of the worst sort!

"Admiring your spots, *nee'ka*," the deepest voice she'd ever heard rumbled out. It was rich and dark, and his voice carried the smallest hint of reverberation, as if she were listening to him through a musical synthesizer.

Giselle discarded that thought as her lips pinched together. It occurred to her that this was probably not the best time to take offense on behalf of freckled red-heads everywhere, but between yesterday's plans having gone awry and the fact that she was lying—naked!—next to the biggest man she'd ever seen was enough to overset her already frayed nerves. "They are not spots," she seethed. "They are freckles."

"Mmm," the giant murmured, his tongue darting out to lick the freckles in question, "'tis like the goddess, your spots."

"They are not," Giselle repeated slowly, "spots. They are—" It dawned on her that her spots, er, freckles were being lapped at. It also occurred to her that she was speaking in a language that wasn't her own. She sucked in her breath, not certain what to think or do about either situation. "Who are you?" she breathed out. "What are you going to do with me?"

The blonde head surfaced from her chest and his profile slowly turned. She gasped when she saw his familiar glowing blue eyes then gasped again when she beheld for the first time the beauty of his face. Never, not once in all of her life, had she been this close to a man so breathtakingly handsome. That realization caused her to falter a bit, but she quickly regrouped. She supposed even sadistic perverts of the worst variety could be handsome.

Giselle's lips pinched together as she regarded him. She ignored the odd feeling of connectedness she felt toward the giant, a feeling that seemed to deepen the longer she looked at him. She decided she had probably become delirious from the entire sordid ordeal. "Who are you?" she snapped.

One golden eyebrow shot up. "I am King Rem Q'an Tal. And 'tis best do you learn never to speak to your Sacred Mate with such disrespect, *nee'ka*."

"My Sacred Mate?" she said grandly. "A king? Ha!" Her hands flew to her breasts to shield them from his view. "I've never heard of—"

Her eyes widened as the sound of low growling emanated from the giant propped up on his elbow beside her. It registered in her brain that the growl was a familiar one. She had last heard it directly before...

Bloody hell! The freckle pervert is going to stab me with a fork!

Having remembered that Anthony had damn near been blinded by a catapulting eating utensil, Giselle's hands instinctively flew from her breasts to shield her eyes. She whimpered, her mind telling her she was about to die.

The growling immediately stopped. Giselle's eyebrows rose from beneath her hands, wondering at the sudden lack of noise. She thought the situation curious enough to brave a peak from behind her fingers.

Giselle sucked in her breath as she watched—and felt—the giant's tongue curl around one of her jutting nipples. The traitorous thing stabbed upwards into his mouth, causing him to groan as he continued to draw from it. She felt herself grow moist and was both embarrassed and horrified by her body's seemingly innate reaction to him.

"Stop it!" she screeched, her hands flying down to shove his face from her breasts. She shielded them once again from his view—and mouth.

The low growling returned.

Giselle's eyebrows slashed a curious arch over her eyes. He'd growled the last time she'd covered her breasts as well. Realizing what he was about, her lips pinched together as she regarded him severely. "I'm onto your game," she said in a disapprovingly spinsterish tone. "If you think the growling will—*oh my.*"

Giselle's mouth fell open as the growling grew louder, more frenzied, crazed even. She watched in horror as the giant's glowing blue gaze clashed with hers and began to...change. A flick of green, then back to blue, another flick of green, and another. Fast. Faster. *Faster...*

The odd necklace he'd clasped about her neck began pulsing. Green—warning green. His teeth were bared.

Giselle began to panic, her breathing growing labored, sweat breaking out onto her forehead. He was going crazy—she was going crazy. She could feel his emotions so strongly as if they were her own—they *were* her own.

What's happening? she thought hysterically, tears forming in her eyes. Madness—she felt consumed by madness. Loneliness—such grief and overwhelming loneliness. Denied of a Sacred Mate...*denied of a Sacred Mate?*

The growling was so loud. Horrifically, frighteningly loud. She was going insane...*oh god she was going insane.*

Giselle released her breasts and clapped her hands over her ears. Her breathing was harsh, labored. She closed her eyes and began to scream. It was awful. So bloody awful. *Help me!* her mind wailed. *Help* —

The growling ceased. A tongue curled around a nipple and drew it back in.

It took Giselle a suspended moment to realize that the threat to her had passed. It was over.

Taking deep shallow breaths, she slowly opened her eyes and gazed down at the gargantuan-sized male she was pinned beneath, the same one who was lapping contentedly at her nipple. Whatever he was, whoever he was, the giant had bound them together in some sort of an inexplicable, bizarre way.

He lived because she lived, breathed because she breathed, remained sane because she was no longer trying to thwart his need to be close to her. She had all of the answers. She just wished she knew the damned questions.

As if from a distance, Giselle watched the giant palm both of her breasts and draw them together that he might take turns suckling from both of her nipples.

He felt happy, she knew. Happy and calm. She decided to let him stay that way — for now.

Suddenly too exhausted to do anything but sleep, she took a calming breath as her head fell back onto the pillows. It was then that she noticed the ceiling for the first time since she'd awoken. Giselle's eyes narrowed in speculation...then widened in understanding.

She was staring up at a porthole, a porthole much like the ones found in cabins aboard ships. Only it wasn't the familiar oceans of earth that greeted her.

It was outer space.

Chapter 5

Meanwhile, in Sand City on Planet Tryston...

High Lord Cam K'al Ra made his way from the conveyance launching pad toward the inside of the black crystal castle known as the Palace of the Dunes. Although he had been to the emperor's dwelling many times over the years, Cam had not been allowed to set eyes on Kara Q'ana Tal since the year she'd turned thirteen.

Kara, the girl-child he would claim as Sacred Mate on her twenty-fifth birthday, was now seventeen, due to turn eighteen and have her come-out in mere days. 'Twas because of the celebratory feast in honor of her come-out that Cam would be permitted to see her in less than a sennight.

Many a long moon-rising, as he had lain in his raised bed and watched dispassionately as his bound servants and *Kefas* had brought him to climax, Cam had reflected on the girl-child that would soon be his bride. 'Twas around Kara's sixteenth year of life that his thoughts had grown more and more fanciful...and more and more lustful.

What did she look like? What did she smell like? What would her channel taste like—what would it feel like as it milked him of life-force?

Cam had called himself a lecher, horrified he'd entertained thoughts about a girl-child still wearing the *kazi*. But, he thought with a sense of impending fate, when Kara had her come-out she would no longer be wearing a child's clothing. She would be donned in a *mazi*, the attire of a budding young woman, her breasts revealed to his hungry gaze through the transparent top she would be sporting.

When Cam walked through the open corridor and into the great hall carved of black crystal, the first two members of the royal family he spotted were the eldest Q'ana Tal—Zora and Zara. The first-born, fraternal twin daughters of the Emperor and Empress.

The eighteen-year-old High Princesses had already had their come-outs several weeks ago so they were now permitted to mingle amongst the warriors who were invited to dine with the royal family. The girls appeared to be having a good time. The ever-social Zara twirled around and showed off how good she looked in her new *mazi* to a warrior seated at the raised table. The warrior looked as though he was ready to spill his life-force at the mere sight of her young jiggling breasts.

Cam grinned, thinking Gio had best put his wagging tongue back in his mouth before the Emperor noticed his lust and sliced it clean out of his mouth. Gio's lips were but scant inches away from Zara's chest, her long pink nipples stabbing at the nearly transparent green top she wore.

Cam decided 'twas mayhap for the best that the sarong skirt of the *mazi* was not transparent as well, for if poor Gio were able to see Zara's mons, a mons that was no-doubt thatched of the same fire-berry red as the hair on her head, the warrior mayhap would not have been able to stop his life-force from spurting.

Cam waved to Gio, signaling to him with a nod and a grin that they would speak later, then continued his stride across the great hall. 'Twas barely a Nuba-second later when his eyes at last settled upon the royal couple themselves, Emperor Zor and Empress Kyra.

The Empress looked radiant today, the transparent *qi'ka* she wore a shimmering black. Her breasts were fully engorged, evidence that the Emperor had not been able to abstain from gorging whilst mating with his beautiful *nee'ka* for the requisite number of Yessat years that would allow for her sweet juice to dry up. The royal Sacred Mates now boasted of seven children, the eldest being Zora and Zara, the youngest being two-year-old Jun.

As Cam drew closer he realized that the royal couple was arguing over one of their children. Curious as to whether their conversation revolved around Kara, his ears perked up. But nay, he thought with a certain amount of disappointment, it was not of his future Sacred Mate they spoke. 'Twas of twelve-year-old Jor, the High King of planet Tryston, the sacred title having been conferred upon the eldest Q'an Tal male at birth.

"I think," Kyra said distinctly, her words spaced for emphasis, "that giving Jor a harem for his birthday next month is a bit much. Good grief Zor, he's still a boy!"

The Emperor sniffed at that. "'Tis not true, my hearts. On Tryston a boy becomes a man when he reaches his thirteenth Yessat year." Zor waved a hand about dismissively. "You forget that did Jor live on your primitive earth, he would be turning one hundred and thirty years old next month."

Kyra rolled her eyes. "We're not on earth, we're on Tryston. And if you want to look at things like that then why not give Zora and Zara a male harem?" She smiled sweetly and utterly falsely. "They are, after all, one hundred and eighty years old back on earth."

The twins giggled, having overheard their mother's words. "Aye papa," Zara called out with a grin. "I think *mani* has the right of it."

A tic began to work in the Emperor's cheek. "I will not listen to this blasphemy from any of you." His hand slashed through the air. "Leastways, all of my girl-children shall go to their Sacred Mates with virgin channels."

Cam nodded, agreeing completely. He would kill any warrior that dared to touch wee Kara.

"Oh?" Kyra said shrilly. "And you call that fair?"

"Aye!" Zor barked. "'Tis fair for a certainty!"

"How so?"

"'Tis fair because I say 'tis fair and I am the Emperor." His hand made another slashing motion. "Jor is a warrior grown next month and he has the need of tight channels to spurt his life-force into."

Kyra's hands flew to her hips. Her nostrils flared. "I give up! There's no talking to you!"

Zor reached down and sifted through her transparent *qi'ka* skirt, parting it open and offering an arousing view of the thatch of fire-berry curls betwixt her thighs to the warriors currently dining around them. He ran his fingers through the sleek pelt, then down lower until he found the Empress' clit. In the way that Trystonni warriors are taught from boyhood to calm the tempers of their wenches, he began stroking her woman's bud in a circular motion, arrogant male satisfaction in his expression when her eyes began to glaze over.

A mated High Lord dining at the raised table with his son instructed him to pay heed that he might learn from the Emperor how to calm a wench. The boy nodded and watched.

"You know a warrior's appetite, *nee'ka*," Zor murmured, his fingers taking her toward climax. "Our son has the need to work out his lust. Surely you can find it in your hearts to grant him that."

The Empress conceded on a barely-stifled groan, her nipples jutting out as she reached her woman's joy.

"Good *pani*." The Emperor petted her downy pelt before returning her *qi'ka* to it's normal position, then ran both of his large hands over her engorged breasts and massaged her nipples. "The bound servants and *Kefas* we give to Jor shall number fifty. Let us belabor the point no more."

Just then the High King Jor made his way into the great hall, his seven foot tall stature bound to gain another several inches before he became a warrior full grown in two fortnights. He was the mirror image of his father, dark hair plaited off the temples in a series of three braids, his eyes the Q'an Tal glowing blue. He bowed to his parents, then bent to kiss his mother on the cheek. "Good morn, *mani*. You look lovely today."

Kyra smiled up to her son, then stood on tiptoe to embrace him. "And you look very handsome. Where have you been?"

"Kara and I were playing a game of *tizi*. 'Twas good fun."

Zor chuckled. "However did you get the imp to agree to play that game? She's never had a care for it for a certainty."

Jor grinned. "I allowed her to model the *mazis* you purchased for her come-out." He rolled his eyes. "I helped her choose the one I thought most fetching, so she agreed to play a game of *tizi* for my trouble."

Cam's jaw clenched. He realized 'twas ridiculous to become jealous of his future bride's brother, yet did he not have a care for Jor to see Kara's perky young breasts, especially when he himself had not yet seen them. By the sands, he groaned, he had best get his possessiveness under control else would it be a terribly long seven Yessat years.

"Cam!" the Empress Kyra exclaimed as she beamed a smile his way. He smiled back as he strode the distance that separated them, inclining his head respectfully when he reached her. "How have you been?"

"I've been well, Your Majesty," he said with a grin. Inclining his head to the Emperor he asked, "And how have the deuce of you fared?"

Zor thumped him affectionately on the back, having long ago come to terms with the fact that his daughter would be mated with the warrior who had already reached the status of High Lord. The Emperor held no doubts but that his future son-within-the-law would become a lesser king within the next four or five Yessat years, mayhap sooner. Cam was the finest of hunters. "We have all been well. 'Tis glad I am that you could make it here in time for Kara's come-out."

"I wouldn't have missed it for all the sands in Tryston," he murmured.

Zor's eyebrows shot up as he considered Cam. "I am well aware of the fact that on the moon-rising of her come-out she belongs to you by the Holy Law and you may visit with her whenever you wish to do so," he said matter-of-factly. "But you must remember 'tis against the Laws of Succession to join with Kara's body until she is of a claimable age which is why, in the interest of helping you retain your sanity, she will continue to dwell in the Palace of the Dunes with her birth family."

Cam nodded his understanding.

Zor lowered his voice, bending toward the younger warrior that his *nee'ka* might not overhear. "And I trust you will be smart enough to have your needs seen to on each occasion before visiting with her, hm?"

"Of course, Excellent One."

Zor nodded. "As I thought. I've sent ten lusty bound servants and ten more of my favored *Kefas* to your apartments that your comforts may be seen to as needed."

Cam inclined his head in thanks. "'Tis much welcomed after so long a journey."

Zor clapped him on the back. "Retire then to your chamber. We shall see you the soonest for the morning repast."

Five Nuba-minutes later, Cam summoned his warrior's garb from his body as he entered his rooms. Making his way toward the bedchamber he was taken aback by the sight that greeted him. "Mara," he murmured, his eyes raking over the naked flesh of the first bound servant he'd ever owned, the very one he had released from servitude more than thirteen Yessat years past. "What do you here?"

"I was recaptured," the blonde explained as she took his erect cock into her warm palms. "The Emperor owns me again," she said with a grin, "but I am yours to use as you see fit whilst you remain in Sand City."

Cam picked her up and impaled her body on his shaft in one smooth motion. He groaned, her channel a tempting repast after not having indulged in it in nigh unto fourteen Yessat years. "I see your channel still drips for me," he ground out as he carried her to the high bed.

"Aye," she whispered, wrapping her legs around his waist and clinging to him as he fell onto the bed and began thrusting into her.

A second bound servant removed her *qi'ka* skirt and joined them on the raised bed, her thighs splayed wide for the High Lord. Cam buried his face in her channel and lapped lustily at her wet flesh whilst his cock continued to impale Mara.

Chapter 6

It had been nearly two full moon-risings since Rem had explained the way of things to Giselle and still he could not coax his *nee'ka* from her rooms. His teeth gritting, he prowled towards their bedchamber aboard his gastrolight cruiser, five gorgeous bound servants and four lusty *Kefas* in tow.

She refused to wear a *qi'ka* in front of Lord Death, that being her main reason for burrowing away. She refused to join Rem in the bathing chamber with the *Kefas*, claiming it was appalling to think he owned slaves. She had refused him this and refused him that, refused even to learn how to pleasure him.

Well no more. 'Twas time to take his high-spirited *nee'ka* in hand and teach her once and for all who was lord and master here. The wee wench had best quit refusing direct orders, and, he thought with a snarl, she had best quit pinching those bedamned intoxicating lips of hers together as though he were a recalcitrant child.

Spots or no spots, Rem would be beguiled by her beauty no more. She would need to join with him on the next moon-rising, so he thought it prudent did she know his body more intimately before breaching her.

And she would, he thought grimly, come out of her rooms and wear her *qi'ka* to the evening repast with Death this moon-rising. He wanted for his best friend to meet his beloved *nee'ka*. And, he arrogantly admitted, he was also of a mind to show off her spots, wanting Death to behold the glory of her *migi*-candy breasts. 'Twas a king's right to show off his spoils.

Rem's shaft grew painfully rigid as his thoughts turned to that of his spotted *nee'ka*. 'Twas time to take his wee wench in hand and teach her the joys of seeing to his needs.

* * * * *

Giselle's lips pinched together in disapproval as she fingered through the alleged clothing contained within the walk-in closet in her bedchamber. If this just didn't beat all then she didn't know what did, she thought grimly. The *qi'kas* sarong skirts were see-through and showed off her entire left leg clear up to her hip and the shirts were no more than transparent genie tops or sometimes strapless bikini tops that came together in a knot just below her cleavage.

Bloody hell! Can my life get any more wretched!

Disallowed the use of any other clothing, Giselle pulled the whisper-soft *vesha* hide around her body and padded back towards the raised bed. She plopped down onto the edge of it with a weary sigh, agitatedly running her hands through her hair.

This had been, without a doubt, the most emotionally taxing two days of her existence. She had been kidnapped and wed to a seven and a half foot giant who claimed to be a king on some moon named Sypar. She had been forbidden any clothing save the transparent horrors from hell in the closet. She was married to a slaveholder who claimed all of his slaves were enchanted, having no thought processes as they had been formed of colored *trelli* sands from the borderlands of the planet Tryston — wherever in the hell that was.

As if all of that were not overwhelming enough, she thought moodily, she could not even retain her modesty and shield her body from Rem's exploratory hands and tongue. Each time she attempted to do as much the big baby commenced his damned growling, his eyes flicking back and forth to that frightening green. Worse yet, she couldn't even be angry with the lecher about it because she knew his emotions were genuine and he truly felt as though he was slipping into the abyss of madness when she shied away from him.

Giselle shook her head slightly and sighed, remembering all of the occasions during the past two days when she had been obliged by sheer fright and worry over the big ogre to pop a nipple into his mouth to calm him. It was the only course of action that seemed to soothe him enough to stop the growling.

Bloody hell! I'm playing mum to a seven and a half foot tall giant with a freckle fetish!

And now, on top of every other oddity she'd been forced to endure as of late, the freckle pervert wanted her to dine with his best friend tonight wearing nothing save one of those wretched *qi'kas*.

Giselle snapped out of her musings as the door to the bedchamber slid open and her alleged husband came strolling in with a determined look in his glowing blue eyes. She swallowed roughly, wondering what that meant precisely.

She wasn't given any time to reflect on that worry for a second later a bevy of busty beauties strolled in behind him and began removing his clothing. Giselle's heart plummeted at the sight of so many chesty women. She felt entirely inadequate when she considered the smallness of her own bosom. Her lips pinching together, she told herself she did not care. Let Rem have as many women as he wanted so long as he left her alone.

She winced at the sound of their amorous giggling, five of the busty women completely topless and wearing only the transparent skirt of the *qi'ka*. They shed those moments later and rubbed their ample breasts up against Rem's body, now as naked as the four glittering women she could only assume were *Kefas* because of their vibrant, shimmery coloring.

Rem plucked at the nipples of one servant, his large fingers running through the golden pelt on the mons of another one. Giselle's back stiffened, jealousy consuming her despite her best attempts to thwart it. She should not care, she told herself bitterly. She did not want to care.

Rem met her gaze and arrogantly cocked a golden eyebrow as if daring her to gainsay his right to do as he would. "You will learn how to pleasure my body this moon-rising, *nee'ka*, that you might be prepared for the joining on the morrow."

Giselle's eyes narrowed at her husband. How dare he call her wife, *nee'ka*, while allowing so many female hands to fondle him.

"Following the joining 'tis your duty as my Queen and Sacred Mate to spend the whole of your days pleasing me in all that you do..."

She harrumphed, her arms crossing over her breasts, which were still concealed by the *vesha* hide.

"...Your every thought will be of how to see to my comforts, your every action a display of your submissiveness to your King and his will."

Giselle's nostrils flared wickedly as she regarded him through narrowed eyes. How dare he speak of himself in the third person! "I think you've enough submissive women around here to see to your needs as you put it.

Why can't you just leave me the bloody hell alone?" she wailed. "Why will you not just take me back to earth as I have begged you repeatedly?"

Rem's hearts sank, a small wounded sound emitting from the back of his throat. Giselle winced, knowing his emotions, her bridal necklace transmitting the feelings of pain and abject loneliness to her. She gritted her teeth, hating that she felt guilty, hating that she cared so much.

"Because you are the only woman I shall ever love, my hearts." His murmur was gentle, at complete odds with the determination emanating from him. "The only woman biologically capable of granting me happiness and hatching my heirs."

Hatching his heirs? Bloody hell!

"And what of my happiness?" she inquired shrilly. "Do you think it makes me happy to see these naked women fondle you?" Her face colored slightly, having realized she had shown him her jealousy, more than she had wanted for him to know that she felt.

Rem appeared startled. "I told you already that I would never know another channel once joined with you." He slashed a hand through the air and gritted his teeth. "You think to distract me from the mission at hand, but it will not work. We shall join on the morrow, *nee'ka*, so 'tis best do you learn how to give me pleasure anon."

Giselle merely harrumphed again.

He wagged a finger at her. "You mayhap think you are too fine of form for a warrior such as myself, and mayhap you have the right of it..."

She could only gawk at him. He was a golden god.

"...Nevertheless," he sniffed, "I am your Sacred Mate." His jaw clenched hotly as he repeatedly jabbed a finger in her direction. "I own each and every spot that graces your wee body. 'Twill be a passing fair day do you accept and submit to my lust."

She shook her head and sighed. She truly didn't understand what the fixation on her freckles was about. If he played connect-the-dots one more time on her cleavage she was liable to murder him.

Giselle gasped as the *vesha* hide was telekinetically summoned from her body, giving her no time to worry over a reply. Her hands flying over her breasts to shield them from so many eyes, she screeched in surprise when his glowing blue gaze pried her hands away from her chest and forced them above her head. Her body was thrust back onto the pillows next, her legs splayed wide, displaying her labia to all and sundry.

Rem grunted in arrogant warrior satisfaction. "My *Kefas* and bound servants will see to your pleasure whilst you watch and learn how to please me." His hand slashed tersely through the air. "Spotted or no', I am your King and master in all things."

Giselle's eyes narrowed as she opened her mouth to curse him. He held up a hand and forestalled her screeching, telekinetically summoning her vocal cords to lock.

Bloody hell! He was a dead man!

Two bound servants and two *Kefa* slaves climbed up onto the raised bed. All four of the women sported breasts the size of watermelons, their areolas large and puffy, their nipples jutting out from the bases. The two bound servants were blonde-haired and possessed golden-brown skin tones. The two *Kefas* were glittery of color, one a glistening green and the other a shimmering violet.

One of the bound servants, a beautiful blonde with breasts so large that they hung fully to her navel, worked her way behind Giselle and pillowed her with her gargantuan-sized chest. She felt the back of her head sink into the soft flesh, a nipple jutting out from behind at either side of her face.

Bloody hell.

Giselle mentally moaned as the mouths of the *Kefas* found her nipples and began to suckle from them. The other busty bound servant lowered her face between Giselle's legs and began to lap at her, her tongue running about the sleek folds of her labia.

Her eyes glazed over in passion, Giselle watched Rem come up on the raised bed, lift the hips of the bound servant licking hungrily at her, and enter her flesh from behind in one long thrust. The bound servant groaned, vibrating Giselle's clit, which thereby caused her breathing to hitch and grow labored.

It felt good, embarrassingly good. So many tongues, so many hands. Lips plucking her nipples, a tongue flicking at her clit. She moaned aloud, absently realizing that her vocal cords had been released. She could scream. She could tell these women to stop. But she didn't.

"'Tis your sweet channel I shall be rutting in on the morrow," Rem ground out as he impaled the blonde servant over and over, again and again. He met Giselle's gaze as he continued his thrusting. "I've waited more Yessat years than you can imagine for your tight flesh, my hearts. Beginning on the morrow your lusty channel shall milk me of all that I have, bringing me to pleasure as much as my needs dictate."

She grew wetter at his words, the images he provoked shockingly heady.

His thrusting picked up, faster and deeper. The bound servant groaned, vibrating Giselle's clit and causing her to do a little groaning of her own.

"'Tis lucky you are that I thwarted your plans to offer the channel that is mine by the Holy Law to the primitive." His eyes flicked a warning green even as he impaled the servant, his teeth baring slightly. "I would have ripped his hearts out with my bare hands had you milked him of life-force as you will milk me."

Giselle's head fell completely back upon the pillowing breasts. Her breathing was labored and sporadic, her nipples jutting up into the mouths of the *Kefas*. She heard Rem's voice as if from a distance, her orgasm too close to remain lucid. So many tongues, so many hands...

The bound servant gently pillowing her nudged Giselle's head toward the left as the servant used her hand to work her stabbing nipple into the Queen's mouth. Delirious with desire, drunk with pleasure, she accepted the elongated flesh between her lips and latched onto it, sucking from it like a lollipop. So many tongues, so many hands, such a gloriously tight nipple...

"Oh god." Giselle burst, her orgasm ripping through her insides as she groaned against the nipple she resumed suckling from. Her own nipples stabbed up into the suctioning mouths of the *Kefas*, inducing the enchanted slaves to mewl and suckle frenziedly. She was barely given time to come down from one orgasm when she felt another tremor of pleasure building. The blonde between her legs continued to lap at her clit even as she heard Rem's shout of satisfaction when he emptied himself into the beautiful servant's flesh.

Never, not once in all of her thirty-six years, had Giselle imagined herself in such a situation. That thought was quickly discarded as pleasure coiled in her belly and formed a tense knot.

Rem dismissed the blonde servant toying with her clit and, reclining on his elbow between her splayed thighs, used his thumb to rub the piece of flesh into submission himself. Giselle moaned, her eyes glazing over, as she met her husband's gaze.

"'Tis necessary to feel pleasure before being able to give it," he murmured. Lowering his head between her legs, he sipped her clit into his mouth and suckled from it, causing her hips to thrash up off of the bed. He continued to draw from her, his eyes closed in bliss, as two bound servants attended to him, one sucking up and down the length of his shaft, the other sucking in his scrotum.

Rem groaned, his face surfacing from Giselle's labia long enough to murmur another command. "Watch the way that the servants pleasure me, *nee'ka*, for 'twill be your turn the soonest."

"Okay," she whispered, more turned on than she'd ever hoped to be. She didn't know how she would feel about everything when the arousal faded, but for now all she could do was bask in it.

She did as she'd been bade, watching Rem's cock disappear into the throat of an extremely talented bound servant. Giselle couldn't imagine ever being able to take so many thick inches all the way in. But the servant didn't seem to mind if the expression on her face was any indication. Her eyes were closed in rapture, her lips curved slightly upward in a smile.

Giselle's breathing grew labored as Rem continued to lick and suck on her clit. She watched through a haze of desire as the servants continued to draw from him, their sucking growing frenzied. He groaned, vibrating her clit. She burst, her hips thrashing about as she came violently for her husband.

Panting heavily, her eyes widened as she watched Rem settle himself between her thighs. His breathing was harsh, his teeth were slightly bared, his eyes flicking back and forth to a glowing green as he grabbed her hips and prepared to thrust into her. He'd obviously experienced more stimulation than he could endure.

Giselle caught her first unimpeded view of his total erection and began to panic. "Please don't!" she cried out, knowing he was far too out of control to take her gently. "Please Rem...*do not*!"

But he was crazed, maddened. The low growling commenced as the predator in him sensed that its mate was trying to shield her body from his dominion. His breathing grew labored and heavy, perspiration broke out all over his body, as he fought the insanity within himself.

Giselle began to cry in earnest, knowing his body would harm hers in his maddened condition, and knowing too that there wasn't a bloody thing she could do to stop him from injuring her. "Oh please," she sobbed, begging him for mercy, "please don't hurt me."

"*Mine*," he growled, his erection poised at the entrance to her vagina, the swollen head seeking out her flesh. His eyes kept flashing back and forth from blue to green and she knew instinctively that he was trying his hardest to fend off whatever it was that was happening to him.

The bound servants began to scream as they flew from the raised bed, making Giselle fully aware of the fact that whatever Rem was turning into was clearly not commonplace on this Sypar where they heralded from. Her fear of her husband turned to anger on behalf of him, genuinely upset that no one had even thought to call out for help as they had fled the room. Her anger gave her renewed strength, strength that she used to calm him.

"Stop this now," she said forcefully, meeting his gaze. Her eyebrows flew up regally. "If you love me as you claim to do then I'm confident you will not harm me."

His eyes continued flicking, his teeth were still bared, but he was beginning to calm down, she realized. She didn't understand how she knew the things she did, but she'd learned over the past couple of days to trust her judgment where this gigantic man was concerned.

She unlatched her nipples from the *Kefas'* mouths and made a shooing motion with her hand, happy to see it had the desired effect as they made their way from the raised bed and walked from the room. Running a soothing hand over her husband's abnormally heated skin, she met his gaze, forcing herself not to react to his growling. "Calm yourself," she said quietly. "I am not trying to shy away from you. I just don't want you to hurt me."

His eyes were still flicking a bit, but they were increasingly staying blue as opposed to the ominous green. His teeth were unbaring and the growling was noticeably lessened.

"It's okay," she murmured, maintaining eye contact. "I promise I will never leave you." She felt a moment's panic at the vow she'd just made, but deep inside she realized he'd never let her go anyway. She didn't comprehend the feeling of connectedness she carried for him or the way she worried over him, but the feelings were there and she went with them. "Just calm down," she said in a soothing whisper, her hand running over his vein-roped forearm.

Rem's breathing was extremely labored, sweat pouring off of him as he continued to fight within himself. His fingers dug into the flesh of her hips, not quite able to let her go.

"I'm never going to leave you," she murmured again. "Not ever."

He fully snapped back into his true self, forcefully relegating the predator within back from whence it had come. Breathing raggedly, he released Giselle's hips and gently came down on top of her. Burying his face in her bosom, he took a calming breath. "What is happening to me, *nee'ka*?" he said hoarsely. "It grows worse and worse."

Giselle sighed deeply as she ran her fingers through her Sacred Mate's long golden hair. "You'll be fine," she promised. "We'll get through this."

We. She'd just made another commitment to him, she realized.

"Nay," he said in a tone so defeated it broke her heart. "I will die the soonest." He took another ragged breath and expelled it. "Mayhap when you have been released from my dominion you will try to think back upon me kindly."

She felt tears forming in her eyes. The thought of his death should have been welcomed, the realization of impending freedom should have delighted any woman in her position, a woman who'd been forced to the Trystonni altar as it were. But both ideas were nothing short of heartbreaking. Her arms tightened around him. "No!" she bit out determinedly. "You will not die."

"*Nee'ka...*"

"No!" Her lips pinched together in resolve. "I know in my heart that there is a way to stop this. We just have to figure out how."

Her words had a calming effect on him. She could feel the rate of his hearts slowing down to a normal beat.

"Now stop all of this ridiculous talk and get some sleep," she said in a matronly manner that would have scared off a lesser man. She pursed her lips as she continued to stroke his mane of silky hair. "I won't even give you a hassle about dining with your best friend when you wake up if you go to sleep just now."

Rem grunted, realizing he was being manipulated but too elated by her concession to argue with her.

"Now," Giselle said grandly, "here's my nipple." She sighed with a dramatic sense of martyrdom. "You best suck on it to keep us from any further episodes." Really, she thought, the lengths she must go to keep him calm! "That's it," she coaxed him as a mother would a child, "pop it into your..."

Her breathing hitched as he drew the elongated bud into the warmth of his mouth and latched onto it. He closed his eyes contentedly as he commenced his suckling. "...mouth," she finished breathlessly.

Rem fell asleep within moments, his entire body exhausted from its earlier fight. Giselle ran her fingers through his hair and sighed, thinking to herself that, ironically enough, the only course of action able to soothe him into a lulling sleep was the very one that guaranteed she'd remain alert and wanting him throughout his entire nap.

Bloody hell! What a damned day!

Chapter 7

The good humor Giselle had been entertaining toward her husband all throughout his nap was quickly put to the test that moon-rising at the evening repast. Rem dismissed her shrewish facial expressions from his mind, his humor too well-restored to worry over it.

Giselle's lips pinched together and her eyes narrowed as her infuriating Sacred Mate pointed out each and every freckle on her shamelessly ill-clad bosom to his best friend, a handsome but frightening looking eight-foot giant with a skull tattooed across his forehead.

Apparently, she thought grimly, this freckle fetish of her husband's was not exclusive to him. The giant named Lord Death gazed at them with lust in his eyes, his jaw slightly lax while ogling Rem's "good fortune".

Bloody hell! How embarrassing!

"This pattern of spots is my favorite," Rem arrogantly announced as he ran a large finger over an array of freckles Giselle had always likened to the Little Dipper. "'Tis enough to cause a warrior to spurt his life-force at the mere looking."

She sucked in her breath, affronted at his nerve.

"Aye," Death rasped out, apparently close to doing a little spurting of his own, "'tis a wondrous pair of *migi-candy* breasts you have claimed." He licked his lips. "Her nipples are fair long as well. Mayhap you would do me the honor of showing off those spoils as well..."

"Absolutely not!" Giselle sputtered, at last finding her voice. "My breasts are not spoils," she gritted out, her arms crossing indignantly over her breasts. "They are—*eek!*"

Giselle's eyes widened in dismay as Rem's low growling commenced. He was so agitated at her instinctive shielding of her breasts that he thoughtlessly knocked over a crystal goblet of *matpow* as he bared his teeth, the glowing turquoise liquid spilling onto the white crystal tabletop. Death appeared alarmed, as though he was worried for his best friend but had no idea what to do.

Giselle frowned at Rem severely, underscoring the fact that she'd had about enough of his insane moments. Really, she thought in exasperation, how much could a woman endure? Picking up her goblet of *matpow*, she hurled the turquoise stuff in her husband's face with a huff. "Stop it!" she screeched. "Bloody hell but I've had enough!"

Rem was so startled that his growling immediately ceased. His breathing was labored and his teeth slightly bared, but he'd regained his sanity enough to regard her.

Giselle surged to her feet. "I will no longer tolerate the baring of fangs in my presence," she sniffed. "Death," she barked, "close your eyes."

"Why?" the giant grumbled out, the skull on his forehead scrunching up.

"Because," she said grandly, her patience wearing thin, "I have to take care of my husband."

Death thought that over for a moment. "I still do not see why 'tis necessary to—"

"Oh bloody hell just forget it!" she fumed. With a strength she didn't even know she possessed, Giselle ripped the *qi'ka* top off of her breasts and popped a nipple into Rem's awaiting mouth. He calmed immediately, his eyes closing in bliss. She rolled her eyes, her face coloring in embarrassment to be doing this in front of someone else.

Bloody hell! Here we go again!

"The *migi*-candy calms him", Death grumbled out in an awe-struck tone of voice. "'Tis a passing fair elixir," he murmured.

Giselle's teeth ground together. She refused to be embarrassed by what could not be helped. "Death!" she snapped.

"Aye?"

"Pass me the *matpow*."

He regarded her solemnly. "I would not be throwing more warrior's brew into his face just now were I you. He appears to be calmed."

Calmed indeed, Giselle thought as her nostrils flared wickedly. He was toying with her nipple like a cat with a delicious new mouse. Flicking it with his tongue, rolling it around between his teeth, sucking on it lustily. "It's not for him," she said, the oddness of the situation at last crumbling her resolve to remain unembarrassed. "It's for me."

"Ah." Death grinned knowingly, the first smile she'd witnessed the giant entertain threatening to erupt into a full-blown chuckle. He stifled it and nodded. "I've just the thing for you, my Queen. 'Tis moonshine from my sector. Sweet as the tit of a *heeka-beast* it is."

Giselle considered the golden-haired giant lapping at her breast and relented with a sigh. "Give me the whole bloody bottle," she muttered.

* * * * *

Twenty minutes later Rem had calmed enough to continue the evening meal, though he had bade Giselle to sit upon his lap that he might fondle her breasts and nipples with ease. She had merely sighed, relenting with slouched shoulders, taking a seat on his lap with the good humor of a woman being led to her own execution.

Eventually, however, after Rem had finger-fed her to the point of satiation, she found her eyelids drifting closed and her body slumping back against her Sacred Mate's in exhaustion. It had been an incredibly long day with so many emotional ups and downs and she was just plain worn out. Downing a bottle of moonshine *matpow* had only further exacerbated her condition.

Rem cradled her against him, his body so large that it was easy for him to cuddle her like an infant. The fingers of his right hand parted her *qi'ka* skirt and he proceeded to gently knead her buttocks as he continued to converse with Lord Death. Giselle purred, not even aware she had done so.

"'Tis Kil's obsession," he said with a sigh. "So long as insurrectionists remain my brother will feel compelled to take them out."

"Aye," Death grumbled. "'Tis the way of it for a certainty." He shook his head. "Though I do not think 'tis healthy to make warring a way of life."

Rem snorted his agreement. "'Tis natural to war when the situation warrants as much, but I sometimes wonder if my brother goes looking for it." He sighed, the feeling of Giselle's buttocks in his palm as soothing as a tranquil balm. Holding her gave his raging emotions more surcease than even the Chief Priestess' tempting channel had been able to grant him. "I have asked the priestesses to pray to the goddess on his behalf. I — *oomph.*"

Giselle abruptly awoke to the unnerving feel of her and her husband being thrown to the floor of the gastrolight cruiser. She held on tightly to his neck, her heart rate picking up when it dawned on her that they were experiencing some manner of mechanical difficulty.

"Oh my god," she stammered out, yelping when the cruiser lurched down another few thousand feet.

Rem held her tightly, his inhuman strength comforting. "Can you make it to the control chamber?" he shouted to Death over the shrill blazing of horns that had begun to sound the moment the gastrolight cruiser had been struck by...something.

"Aye," Death shouted back, his formidable form coming up from the floor. "Give me your hand that I might help you up without your needing to let go of your *nee'ka*. 'Tis safest for all of us in the control room," he bellowed.

Rem held out his hand to Death, the air in the chamber compressing a bit, making it difficult for him to get to his feet. Giselle wrapped her legs around her husband's hips as they slowly ascended, more frightened than she could ever remember being. "What's happening?" she cried out.

"We must make an emergency landing," Rem answered her calmly.

"To where?!" she said semi-hysterically, realizing as she did that they were in the middle of outer space.

"We will know the answer to that when we lock ourselves into the control room, my hearts. Be calm. I will allow no lesser creatures anywhere near you whilst I draw breath."

Giselle gulped, not finding his statement comforting in the slightest. What sort of creatures was he speaking of? she wondered with a sudden light-headedness.

She was given no time to further ponder that horrific thought for Rem was determinedly using his strength to walk against the air currents and make his way from the dining chamber. And he was doing it without even contemplating releasing her. Somewhere in the back of her semi-aware consciousness that action endeared him to her all the more.

They would live through this, she knew. Because of *him*. And if nothing else she would repay him by helping him to find a way to remedy his...problem. Once and for all.

The air began to grow denser and denser as the trio made their way at a snail's pace from the dining hall toward the control chamber. Giselle could hear the heart-wrenching screams of bound servants as they attempted to make their way to the control chamber but, having no warriors to hold onto, were sucked off of their feet by the ungodly pressure and were vacuumed out through holes in the cruiser.

Giselle could only cover her ears and stare in horror, wishing there was something she could do but knowing realistically that she was powerless. Blood and mangled body parts were scattered everywhere, every droplet and each horrific piece being suctioned into outer space one by one through tiny gapes in the cruiser's infrastructure.

And then she saw Yoli, the servant she knew to be Rem's favored from talk amongst his soon-to-be-former harem. Giselle supposed she should have hated the large breasted woman but it was the remembrance of the kindness the beautiful blonde had continually showed to her that made her reach out a hand and shout out a warning to Death as the bound servant was lifted from her feet and began catapulting toward a small gaping hole in the gastrolight cruiser.

Death proved to have lightening-fast reflexes as he whipped a heavily muscled arm out and snatched Yoli in mid-air as though she weighed no more than a trite leaf. The bound servant whimpered and clung to him, the crazed look of a woman who had barely survived death casting her features in horrified relief. Her breasts smashed into Death's chest as she held onto him tightly.

And then somehow, amidst the death and carnage, Giselle soon found herself in the manned control room, the air-tight locks clasping shut with a solid thud behind them. The air in the cabin immediately pressurized, letting everyone know that they were safe, or at least safe for the time being.

Giselle could only close her eyes in relief as Rem set her on her feet and possessively kissed her atop the head. She hugged him tightly, more grateful than she'd ever thought she'd be toward this man.

"'Tis all right, my hearts," he murmured. "You are safe."

Giselle nodded as she sucked in a steadying breath. That had been too close. What if they hadn't made it to the control chamber before—

She let out a cry of surprised pleasure when the very familiar sound of two poodles yipping reached her ears. "Bryony," she breathed out, "and Tess."

The poodles bounded over to the Queen of Sypar, their tails wagging delightedly as she scooped them both up. "Oh how I've missed you!" She buried her face in their fur and inhaled the freshly bathed scent of it, much as she'd done all those lonely nights in Shoreham when her beloved father had lain dying in the room next door.

Giselle planted kisses atop both their fluffy heads, then shot her gaze up to Rem who was watching her every action. She searched his eyes, not quite believing what he'd done. "You brought them," she whispered. "Why?"

"Because I love you," he said simply, softly. "And because my hearts told me you loved them."

Giselle took a deep breath as she continued to search her husband's glowing blue gaze.

It was much worse than she'd originally thought, she conceded. She wasn't just softening towards the big ogre— she was falling in love with him.

Chapter 8

Meanwhile, in Sand City...

Cam jogged towards the battle-planning chamber, slowing down only after he reached it. Walking in long strides he made his way past the warrior-guardsmen and entered the lair of the Emperor. Nodding respectfully, he came to a halt before him. "I've assembled a troop of my finest hunters to scour the fifth dimension for thy brother, Excellent One."

"Good." Zor inclined his head, then motioned for Cam to have a seat at the raised stratagem table. "I'm certain Rem and his *nee'ka* are fine, but I want them found the soonest nevertheless."

"I shall see to it myself, Your Majesty."

"Nay, 'tis not necessary." He waved a dismissive hand. "Leastways, my brother Kil is en route to the fifth dimension as we speak to head up the hunt. 'Tis good for him to take his mind from the insurrectionists for a spell."

Cam nodded as he took his seat but said nothing.

The Emperor sighed, tiredly running a hand through his dark hair. "Kil assured me that he will call upon us should the need warrant, so Kara's come-out will remain on schedule for the present."

Cam stirred in his chair, thinking himself a lecher for getting an erection at his future Sacred Mate's mere name. Especially considering the news report they'd recently received from Rem's cruiser pilot, proclaiming the death toll as a grim one.

Zor raised a knowing brow and chuckled slightly despite the seriousness of the situation. "Do not forget to have your pleasures seen to before joining the celebratory dinner party."

Cam's face colored a bit, but he didn't break the Emperor's gaze. "For a certainty." His thoughts then turned to Kara, the brewing restlessness he was experiencing from knowing he would once again be permitted to clap eyes on her growing in its intensity. By the sands, but how he wished she had already reached a claimable age.

The Emperor flicked his gaze toward Cam as he watched the range of emotions play about his future son-within-the-law's face. "Send out your hunting party anon," he said softly, clapping him on the back.

He stood up to make his exit, leaving Cam to stare after him.

Chapter 9

"Where are we?" Giselle's eyes widened in a curious mix of fright and awe as she firmly clutched Rem's large hand and gawked at the surroundings they were walking into from aboard the soon-to-be-abandoned gastrolight cruiser. "I've never seen anything like this place," she breathed out.

Neither had Rem, but he declined to mention that fact out of worry for her. His poor wee Sacred Mate had been handed an awful lot of new changes as it was without making her fret needlessly. Rem's glowing blue gaze flicked over to Death where his friend was currently bartering with a transparent life-form for directions to the nearest holo-port.

These silicone-based, see-through life-forms were predators, Rem realized. One look at their hideous fangs seen easily through their transparent white-like jaws told him as much.

But they were also intelligent creatures with the capacity for higher language and because of that fact they would not wish to make war with an entire galaxy of warriors, which they had to realize would be precisely what would transpire if they attempted to make a meal of a High Lord, a King, and his Queen. The three of Rem's warrior entourage who had accompanied him on his quest drew protectively around the Queen, *zykifs* in hand.

Rem glanced about, his instincts telling him without confirmation that the planet they had landed on was protected from telekinetic activity by a natural discharge of some type of black smoke that billowed downwards from the planet's triple suns. None of them would be able to engage in telekinetic warfare. 'Twould come down to weaponry and brute strength did the situation warrant such.

"According to the holo-reading," Rem said to Giselle, "we have landed within the fifth dimension on a planet removed from any galactic dominion."

Her eyes shot up to meet his. "We are not in a galaxy?" she whispered in confusion. Her eyes flicked about and she swallowed roughly as she watched a bluish saliva drip from the fangs of a creature whose crimson eyes tracked her every move.

"Nay, we are not within a galaxy. 'Tis difficult to explain, my hearts, but we have landed within a void, a black hole of sorts."

"A black hole," she repeated in low tones, awed in spite of the predator sizing her up. One of the leading scientific theories back on earth, she remembered, was that life could not survive within a black hole. It was presumed that the sheer density of the atmosphere within it would cause immediate death by implosion. Apparently they had been wrong on that score. These transparent creatures were very real, and she and their entourage were still very much alive...for now.

"What do you mean by the latter part of your explanation?" Giselle asked, her nose wrinkling. "You said a black hole *of sorts*. What do you mean by *of sorts*?"

Rem half-snorted and half-chuckled, thinking it an odd time to question him. "This planet exists within a wormhole which in turn is hosted within a black hole." He nodded. "So you see, my hearts, 'tis not a black hole in and of itself, but 'tis the wormhole within it that this planet dwells in."

Ever the straight-A student, Giselle nodded her understanding. The excitement she emitted was a tangible thing. "So it's true that wormholes exist," she murmured, her green eyes round. She reflected back upon that scientific theory as well, remembering wormholes to be shortcuts in outer space that many back on earth believed would allow for journeys at speeds faster than light from one galaxy or dimension to the next. "That's incredible."

Rem shrugged, having known as much all of his Yessat years and therefore finding nothing remarkable about it.

Bryony and Tess began to whine at Giselle's heels, inducing her to release her husband's hand and pick them up. They were shivering, she noted, and when her gaze met that of a salivating predator's, she realized why. The translucent creature might be wizened enough to leave alone the warriors, and her and Yoli because they were being protected by them, but it would think nothing of snuffing out the lives of her tiny poodles.

"There's a holo-port a moon-rising's journey from here," Death grumbled as he strode back toward the group. "'Twill not take us far, I fear, but 'twill at least take us a planet over where the predators hold no dominion."

Rem nodded, realizing that if semi-humanoid life existed the next planet over they were likely to have a holo-port that could transport them back into the seventh dimension. If not they would hopefully at least have a gastrolight cruiser up on the auctioning block.

"Which way do we set out?" Rem asked calmly, his eyes flicking a warning green at the predator who dared drool over his *nee'ka*. He grunted with satisfaction when the creature backed off, clearly recognizing his potential for violence.

"West," Death rumbled out, waving a hand in said direction, "toward the smallest of the suns." He drew Yoli into his side, a large hand running over her breasts then settling to tweak at her nipples.

Rem's eyes flicked dispassionately over Yoli's fertile form, growing heated only when his gaze settled upon his *nee'ka*. He told himself it was no time for his lust, that he could taste of her charms later whilst they were bedded down for the eve. He glanced back to Death. "I have not a care for the way in which that bizarre red fog rises up from the ground here."

"Aye," Death seconded, "the red mist serves to shield whatever creatures might lurk beneath it."

Giselle sucked in her breath at his words, unconsciously burrowing into Rem's arms as she did so. Her gaze flicked down to the ground in question as she realized for the first time that not only was she unable to see for the red fog at her feet, but the ground was shifty, as if made of a gel-like substance.

She bit her lip, wondering at the bizarre world she was in. As far as the eye could see there was nothing to look at but billowing black smoke descending from the heavens and red mist rising up as if paying homage to it.

Beyond that there was nothing but a dense atmosphere that was quite dark as a result of the black smoke, and transparent predators with hideous fangs. She looked as far to the west as was possible, concluding that their journey would be a long one for she wasn't able to make out any structures within a close proximity.

Deep in thought, Rem was frowning as he glanced back at his warrior entourage. "You two keep your weapons readied at all times for we know not what we are up against." At their nods, he turned to the third warrior. "And I want you to see to my *nee'ka's* wee pets."

Giselle didn't like releasing Bryony and Tess to the giant, but knew she didn't have a choice. She relented with a soft sigh. They'd be safer with an armed warrior anyway.

Rem turned next to face Death. "We've some leathers we can strap the wenches to — "

Giselle's eyebrows rose.

" — that they might not be forced to walk upon this shifty ground."

She sighed a breath of relief.

Death nodded and within minutes the two warlords had fashioned together harnesses that would secure the women against their chests. Giselle let out a surprised little yelp as she was plucked from the ground and put inside of a grouping of leather-like straps that had been tied together in an unforgiving knot around Rem's back.

It occurred to her as her body snuggled into the comforting strength of her Sacred Mate's chest that she should probably take offense at being slung inside of a papoose much like an infant being carted around at the fair by its father. But, quite frankly, she was too happy to be off of the gel-like ground to give such a thought more than a passing nod.

Yoli was the next one to be taken up, though she was being secured to Death instead of Rem. Giselle's face colored slightly as she watched the eight-foot giant pop a nipple into his mouth as he harnessed her, his lusty intentions only further encouraged by a purring Yoli. She arched her back and thrust her breasts upward, her eyes closed in bliss as Death suckled from her watermelon-sized bosom.

"Let us begin our trek," Rem said, thinking nothing of the show the bound servant and his best friend were putting on for all and sundry.

"Aye," Death grumbled from around a hard nipple, "I'm right beside you."

Giselle's eyes remained trained on Death and Yoli for the next half-hour of their journey, moisture growing rampant between her legs as she did so. Never in all of her sheltered life had she so much as watched a porn film, let alone played witness to one being carried out in the flesh. She could surmise that Death was bringing the bound servant to orgasm by doing no more than kissing her breasts.

"Remove my cock from my leathers," Death ordered her in low tones. "Then wrap your legs about me."

Yoli semi-complied, freeing his erection and stroking it wantonly.

Death groaned, needing more. "I said to wrap your legs about me. You have been given to me by King Rem—"

Giselle's eyes widened in shock—Rem gave his favorite harem girl away?

"—so 'tis I you now call master."

Yoli needed no further prodding. Closing her eyes in anticipation, she wrapped her legs around the giant's hips and sank down onto his proportionately huge cock with a moan. Giselle felt tremors set off in her own belly as she watched, unable to tear her eyes away from the graphic scene should she want to.

Yoli groaned loudly with each of Death's footfalls, his every step serving to naturally impale her over and over again. Her head fell back as she arched her back and ran her hands over her breasts, tweaking and pulling at the nipples to enhance her desire.

Death groaned as the bound servant's flesh milked him, her orgasms causing her vagina to contract around his rod. For another ten minutes—and on Yoli's part ten orgasms—the erotic scene continued until finally Death grabbed her hips and, slamming into her flesh three more times, spurted himself inside of her with a bellow.

Giselle was so turned on watching them that she offered Rem no resistance when he clutched her hips and began rubbing her clit up and down the length of his erection through the black leather-like pants he wore.

"I've tried to resist touching you until we are attended to by the Chief Priestess following the consummation feast," he murmured. "Yet I cannot stop my arousal whilst near you, my hearts."

Giselle's eyes closed on a breathy sigh as the friction at her clit grew in its intensity. She was going to come. She knew it and for once she didn't care that it was going to happen amongst a group of strangers.

"I need to impale you the soonest," he said hoarsely, working her clit against him in brisk motions that drove her toward orgasm. "I need your tight flesh wrapped about me, milking me for all that I have."

"Oh god."

Giselle came on a loud groan, her nipples jutting up against the see-through fabric of the purplish *qi'ka* top she wore. Rem bent his neck to suckle at one, a low growl resonating in the back of his throat when he realized the strapless bikini-top was impeding him from what he needed.

Instinctively, without so much as a pause, Giselle reached up and unknotted the top, freeing her nipples to his awaiting mouth. She sucked in her breath as he took one in and drew from it, her strawberry-blonde hair cascading down as she bared her neck to him.

Giselle gloried in the feel of his mouth latched onto her, knowing in her heart that she no longer carried a reticence toward his attention. She was ready to make love with him, and if she was honest with herself, she needed him inside of her as badly as he needed to be there.

* * * * *

Rem suckled from her nipples until he felt calmed, stopping only when he felt able to do so. He continued to play with her body all throughout the next three hours of their journey, repeatedly bringing her to orgasm until she was naught but trembling flesh in his hands. He tweaked at her nipples, ran his fingers reverently over her spots, played with her clit until she reached her woman's joy, over and over again.

By the time the planet was swamped in total darkness and his warriors had located a secured cave-like structure for sleeping, Rem was worked up into a state of need the likes of which he'd never before entertained. There would be no consummation feast, he realized, for he would be joining with his *nee'ka's* wee body this very moon-rising.

"Oh god Rem."

Rem continued to bring Giselle to her woman's joy as he impatiently waited for his warriors to erect an impenetrable leather-like tent for him and his bride to share. Death glanced at him worriedly, conveying his fear that Rem might do his wee wife a harm. Rem subtly shook his head, saying without words that he knew what he was about.

Indeed, Rem thought, as they took to the tent and he lowered Giselle to the ground, he needed not the ministrations of the Chief Priestess as aide, for the bedeviling nipples on his *nee'ka* were far more calming. "'Tis time, my love," he murmured, his eyes feasting on her body as he summoned off her clothing. His soulful gaze swept over her, branding her forevermore as his own. For hundreds of years he had waited upon this one tiny woman, his life an empty abyss without her. He could wait no longer to join them together, not even a day.

"I'm ready," she whispered back, reaching out for him, wanting his body to cover hers. She gazed up at him expectantly, more thankful than she could say that this handsome giant had thwarted her plans to bed the horrid Anthony. Her virginity would not be claimed by a pasta-inhaling wimp, she thought with an inward smile, but by a man perfect of face and form. What's more, he was the man she was in love with. She wasn't quite ready to admit aloud such a heady emotion, but she recognized it for what it was.

Rem groaned as he came down on top of her, kissing her breasts as he settled himself between her thighs. His tongue traced over the spots he so much adored as he poised the swollen head, already wet with pre-ejaculate, at the opening of her channel. Not wanting to give her time to experience a virgin's doubts, or to give the predator within him time to come out, he impaled her with one long thrust, ripping through her hymen as she screamed.

'Twas done. He was fully embedded. Once he climaxed within her they would be fully mated.

"*Shh*, my hearts," he whispered thickly as he began to gently move within her. He gritted his teeth at the exquisite tightness, the milking flesh that had been made by the goddess to service him and only him so pleasurous it was painful.

Giselle forcefully calmed herself, knowing his intentions had been pure. She could feel his emotions, knew he had meant only to get the hardest part over and done with, much the way a parent might rip a band-aid from a child's wound rather than take it off in torturously slow tears.

As her pain began to lessen, the pleasure began to build. Running her hands over his sweat-slicked back muscles, she soothed him with her touch in a way only she was capable of doing. She could feel the intensity within him, understood through his emotions the super-human control he was exerting in order to keep from rutting on her like a crazed animal. He needed her with a ferocity she would never be able to fully comprehend, his hundreds of years long nightmare at last drawing to an end.

"Oh *nee'ka*," Rem said hoarsely as he moved in and out of her wet flesh in long, deep strokes, "'tis sweet bliss, your channel."

Giselle's eyes glazed over at his words. She reached up and ran a soothing hand over his clenched jaw. "Am I doing it right?" she asked seriously. She closed her eyes briefly as his cock hit a particularly sensitive spot.

"Aye," he ground out, picking up the pace of his thrusts. "'Tis naught in the whole of existence that could feel better."

Her head fell back on the *vesha* hides as Rem continued to mount her. She sensed that his control was a tenuous thing, becoming more and more threadbare as they continued to couple. His emotions were screaming with the need to climax, the primal part of him wanting to dominate and lay claim for all times. She decided then and there to give him what he wanted — what he needed. She arched her hips and surged upwards.

Rem groaned as beads of perspiration formed on his forehead. "Do not," he bit out, "go faster. 'Tis all I can endure to keep from rutting in you as it is." His voice was harsh, wanting her to realize the all-consuming level of his lust, needing her to understand that the sweet torture was already nigh unto killing him.

But Giselle paid his words no heed as she wrapped her legs around his waist. "Then rut in me," she said thickly, her hips rearing up in a gesture that was as submissive as it was brazen. "I want everything."

It was all the coaxing Rem needed. With a loud groan he buried himself to the hilt, impaling the flesh he now owned by the Holy Law over and over again in deep, rapid thrusts.

"Oh my god." Giselle moaned like a wanton as he pounded deep within her, for once neither of them afraid of his dominating side. They basked in it, reveled in it, as he allowed himself free reign on the woman he'd coveted for a lifetime.

"'Tis mine," he ground out, his nostrils flaring as he impaled her over and over, again and again. The sound of her flesh enveloping him was an added aphrodisiac. "I command you to tell me now that this channel belongs to me."

Giselle could only moan as his thrusts grew more rapid, more penetrating.

"Tell me."

"Yes," she groaned, realizing the importance of the words to his state of mind, "I belong to you."

He grunted arrogantly, thrusting deeply again and again. He rotated his hips and plowed into the most sensitive spot of her channel. "Prove it. Milk me."

Giselle screamed out in pleasure as a violent orgasm ripped through her belly. Her vagina contracted rapidly around his shaft, milking him as he'd demanded.

Rem bellowed his orgasm throughout the cavern, the overpowering pleasure more than he'd ever imagined to one day feel as he spurted himself inside of her flesh.

Giselle's eyes widened as her bridal necklace began to rapidly pulsate and a near-maddening euphoria overwhelmed her body. She and Rem shouted out together, both of their bodies convulsing in the most painful pleasure imaginable as a series of relentless orgasms tore through both of them.

It was long minutes before they were calmed down from their love-making, longer minutes before their breathing returned to normal.

Giselle fell asleep with a smile on her face, the feel of a warm tongue curling about her nipple striking her as the most natural feeling in the world.

Chapter 10

The following morning in the realm of
Q'i Liko Aki Jiq —
She Who Is Borne of the Goddess...

After having lived out eighteen Yessat years of life on Tryston, the Empress Kyra no longer thought anything of situations that would have made her balk when she'd been a new arrival to the planet. Running her tongue about the slick labial folds of the Chief Priestess, her breathing grew labored with arousal when Ari came on a groan, her climax causing her puffy pink nipples to jut upwards. Kyra's face surfaced to lap at them, drawing them into her mouth to sip from them for long minutes.

And then it was Kyra's turn to feel pleasure as Ari nudged her gently down onto her back and buried her perfect face in the Empress' engorged breasts. She sucked on her nipples until Kyra was ripe for the plucking, only then going lower to feast on her channel.

Kyra convulsed on a groan, causing Ari to smile. The Chief Priestess ran her nose and lips through the silky pelt of fire-berry hair covering the Empress' mons, understanding why the Emperor was so bedeviled by it. 'Twas soft to the touch and of exquisite coloring.

Drawing herself up to recline next to Kyra on her elbow, Ari ran her hand over her friend's breasts as she regarded her. "What brings you here today?" Her grin was as impish as it had been the day the two women had first met. "Leastways 'tis not just the lure of my tongue for a certainty."

Kyra grinned back, her hands falling over her head to rest while Ari massaged her breasts and nipples. She sighed in satisfaction, a smile of contented bliss enveloping her face.

Eighteen Yessat years ago Kyra had often times found herself wondering why it was that Trystonni females remained loyal to their friends. Save a few bad seeds scattered about here and there, there was never the cattiness or back-stabbing that could be found amongst earthling females.

A few years later the Empress had made the realization on her own concerning why Trystonni women were so different from the females found back on earth. The women of this planet were, to put it bluntly, too busy peaking together to give credence to trivial things like cattiness. What started out in baths with *Kefas* soon evolved into lustier sport.

"I wouldn't bet on that," Kyra grinned, her thighs automatically parting when she felt Ari reach down to stroke her clit, "you have a pretty talented tongue."

The Chief Priestess chuckled as she rubbed the Empress' clit in a slow circular motion. "Tell me what troubles you, my friend."

Kyra sighed resignedly, realizing it was time to fess up. She met Ari's eyes as the Chief Priestess stroked her into arousal. "It's Jor, my son." She took a deep breath. "Try as I might I can't seem to warm up to the idea of him being given a harem at the age of thirteen."

"Ah," Ari murmured, understanding her friend's position for they'd been over this ground before. "I should hope that by now you've come to realize that a Trystonni at thirteen is not the same as an earthling at thirteen."

"Yes but—"

"Aye but nothing." Ari shook her head slightly. "'Tis true that female children are not women full grown at thirteen, but 'tis not the way of it for a male. At thirteen a

Trystonni male is a man, his thought processes as complex as any other adult's, his age on your earth over one hundred years old."

Kyra's lips pinched together. "I don't get it. Why would a male child evolve more rapidly than a female child?"

Ari shrugged. "Nature deemed it necessary that warriors might defend the women of their line from a young age." She looked at her pointedly. "You have witnessed over the Yessat years the carnage that has been a direct result of the insurrectionists. Can you imagine what would have become of our women had we no warriors for protection?"

Kyra conceded to that. "True." She chuckled self-depreciatingly. "But I'm still having a difficult time accepting the fact that my baby boy will be a full-grown man within the month."

Ari smiled as she rubbed the Empress' clit. "I think all *manis* feel the same. However," she said determinedly, "you must realize that in this instance your Sacred Mate has the right of it. Jor has needs that must be seen to."

Kyra sighed but said nothing.

Ari plowed onwards. "Already the High King is being advised by lesser priestesses."

Kyra arched one fire-berry brow. "Advised?"

"Sucked off," the Chief Priestess clarified.

"I was afraid of that."

Ari giggled. "Would you have your poor son die of a bursting man sac?"

Kyra groaned, the mental image as unpleasant as the idea of Jor being *advised*.

"'Tis just a suckling the lusty High King gets now," Ari assured her, "no wench shall mount him till the moon-rising of his thirteenth Yessat year."

"I just hope I can reconcile myself to this by the time that auspicious day rolls around," she said dryly.

"You will," Ari said firmly. "Over the course of the next few weeks you will take notice of rapid evolvements in Jor's thought processes and body. His height will spurt another six inches or so, his body will become more heavily muscled, and on the moon-rising of his birthday you will harbor no doubts but that your son is a warrior full grown."

Kyra nodded, hoping it would be as her good friend had said. Resigning herself to the inevitable, she brushed the worries from her mind and concentrated on the orgasm fast approaching.

Chapter 11

When yet another relentless orgasm tore through her belly, Giselle didn't know whether to laugh or cry. The group had been trekking for over four hours and according to Death they were very close to the holo-port.

Throughout the entire four hour journey through the red mist and black smoke, Giselle had been up in her papoose, impaled on her husband's shaft. Rem had made it very clear with a bit of growling and eye color shifting that it was no longer acceptable for her body to be disjoined from his so long as it was possible to couple.

And so she had complied, not wanting to cause him any emotional anguish, especially considering the fact that he needed to stay calm and alert in case any surprises should befall their group of seven.

Every step Rem took, however, was maddening in the extreme. The impalements were hard and managed to hit the most sensitive spot within her quivering vagina every time without fail. She kept coming and coming and every few times that she burst Rem would join her in orgasm, which only caused her bridal necklace to pulse and her orgasms to become so intense that the pleasure bordered on the painful.

If multiple erections were any indication, then the warriors walking beside them certainly seemed to appreciate the never-ending show. Their eyes continually flicked to Giselle's *migi*-candy breasts, her freckles apparently an aphrodisiac to all of them.

Bloody hell! What was with that?

At last, unable to endure another orgasm without going insane, Giselle wrapped her arms tightly around Rem's neck to steady herself...and to keep her body from being impaled so deeply. "Rem," she panted, her hair damp with perspiration, "I beg you to put that thing away. You're liable to kill me if we keep this up."

The low growl began. Giselle's lips pinched together as she whacked him soundly on the chest. "Stop it!" she shrieked. "All the growling in the world won't change my mind just now. I need some food and drink."

Rem immediately stopped growling, his appearance almost contrite. He sighed deeply. "I cannot bear to be disjoined from you just yet, my hearts. Leastways I will hopefully be feeling up to releasing you in another few hours—"

"A few hours?" she sputtered.

Bloody hell! She'd be a quivering corpse outside of a few minutes!

"Rem," she wailed like a martyr, "I have honestly reached the limit of my endurance." Her hand flew dramatically to her brow, showing him her palm. "Can you not compromise on this?"

He grunted, clearly not having a care for her plan. In the end, however, his desire for her comfort won out over his need to be milked. "Alright," he gritted out, "I will allow for a compromise." He wrapped his arms tightly about her so that their bodies were not disjoined but so also that his Sacred Mate was not constantly impaled to the point of madness. "Is this more to your liking?"

Giselle sighed, realizing it was the biggest concession she was likely to get. She supposed it wasn't so bad. She was still filled with him, there was still some friction down there, but it was more of a languid ache than a sharp yearning.

That knowledge, however, didn't keep her lips from pinching together or her nostrils from flaring. "I shall have to nominate you for the Sacred Mate of the year award," she declared grandly. Her arms flew out in her greatest display of drama yet. "Pilgrims will trek from galaxies far and wide to behold the glory of King Rem Q'an Tal, Sacred Mate extraordinaire."

He took offense at her mocking tone. "You have the right of it for a certainty," he sniffed. "'Tis a passing fair day when a *nee'ka* realizes the glory of her good fortune."

She could only harrumph.

* * * * *

An hour later, as Giselle watched a warrior point a *zykif* at a five hundred pound translucent snake-like creature that had wrapped itself around Death's legs and was preparing to squeeze the life out of him, she could only be grateful that she was in her papoose.

The pulse of energy that beamed out of the weapon burned the fanged, twelve-legged creature into a crisp upon contact. Death merely shrugged the charred remains off of his body, gave a small nod of thanks to the warrior that had intervened on his behalf, then continued on as though nothing out of the ordinary had happened, his large hands palming Yoli's buttocks and kneading them.

Giselle bit down hard on her lip as she and Yoli exchanged worried looks. If there had been one of these creatures, then there could be more.

Suddenly the fact that she was still impaled on Rem seemed more of a blessing than anything. She decided not to argue with him when he released her body to point towards the holo-port in the distance, allowing her to be re-impaled as the warriors walked briskly toward the structure.

Giselle cried out on a moan as an orgasm rippled through her body. Rem came to a halt within the holo-port structure and, after flicking one of her distended nipples back and forth a few times, raised her *qi'ka* top over her breasts. "I would not have outsiders to think you a bound servant," he said in the way of explanation.

"Shall I get out of the papoose?" she asked breathlessly, still coming down from her last climax.

His arms tightened around her. "Nay. Not until we know what we're up against."

She knew that might have been one of his reasons, but the main one was that he simply didn't want to be disjoined from her body.

And so it transpired that an armed warrior went through the transport first, followed by Rem, Death, and the women they carried. The rear was brought in by the warrior who carried Bryony and Tess and a final armed warrior at the very back.

One minute Giselle had been in a black and red pit, but the next, an invisible barrier later, she found their group spit out onto a beautiful purple planet that Rem recognized as a sixth dimension realm in the Horon Galaxy. The transport had taken them further than he'd dared to hope.

Rem's gaze flicked towards Death. He smiled over to his best friend as he tightened his hold on Giselle. "'Tis the planet Joo we've landed on my friend. They've a holo-port that leads to the seventh dimension on the other side of the mountainous terrain."

"How long of a journey are we talking?"

"Mayhap a wee fortnight if we are lucky enough to find a hover-craft on the auctioning block."

"And if we need walk?"

Rem sighed. "Months."

Giselle bit down on her lip as she listened to them talk.

A warrior called Var sidled up to Rem and made an announcement as he gauged readings from the small but complex computer-like instrument he carried. "I'm happy to report that Joo is inhabited of goddess-worshippers, so 'tis likely we will find them to be allies fluent in our tongue."

Rem nodded. "I was here a few times as a man-child whilst on goodwill missions with my sire." He grinned. "'Tis likely you will enjoy our stay on Joo."

The warrior raised a brow but didn't question his King. 'Twas Rem's right to further clarify such a statement should he desire it.

"We've only an hour's walk," Rem continued on, "until we come upon the first village." He waggled his eyebrows. "The wenches on Joo are a lusty lot so they do not bother to don clothing..."

The warriors smiled at that knowledge.

"...They will milk your rods for all you have until you've spilled so much life-force 'tis hard to walk." Rem looked pointedly at Giselle as though he was suffering from that very ailment. She merely threw him an *it's-your-fault-not-mine* look.

"I remember when I was a man-child..." Rem waxed nostalgically to the group as a whole whilst he held on tightly to a still-impaled Giselle, "...and I first visited Joo with Kil and my sire." He shook his head slightly and grinned. "It took but one suckling from a wench here to drive me into begging my sire to steal away some of these wenches for the harem I was to be gifted with on the moon-rising of my thirteenth Yessat year."

Giselle's eyebrows shot up. A harem at thirteen? *Bloody hell!*

"But, of course," Rem concluded, "'tis illegal in Trek Mi Q'an Galaxy to make a bound servant of a wench whose planet we are not at war with. So my sire gave me his nay."

The warriors chuckled, enjoying the story. Even Death grinned.

Giselle found her eyes straying to Yoli, wondering not for the first time how she had been captured and what would happen to her upon her release. She could see why the bound servant would be such a highly coveted spoil of war. Yoli was beautiful, busty, and if the way she was stroking Death's shaft and placing kisses all over his torso was any indication, she was also incredibly lusty.

Roughly an hour later, Giselle glanced about in wide-eyed awe of the village of sorts that they were entering. The inhabitants of Joo looked as human as the members of their group, the only noticeable difference being their skin and hair colors which was either a shiny silver, a decadent lavender, or a shimmery combination of both.

And indeed, Rem had been correct about the state of dress on Joo as well. The few males she'd seen were fully clothed, while the females pranced around completely divested of clothing.

The atmosphere here was mostly clear save for a purplish haze that hovered in the skies much like clouds on earth. The trees and vegetation were a bit odd, all of them gargantuan in size and totally silver, covered in purple berries. Such a mechanism of evolution no doubt allowed for the citizens of Joo to find natural camouflage in the jungles should they ever be attacked. Nature, she thought, was an awesome thing.

The building structures, however, were the most fascinating to Giselle for they all appeared to be underground. One small crude doorway formed of purple clay was erected within a clearing in the jungle which, when opened and entered, led to whatever chambers laid below the purple soil.

Rem finally released Giselle from her papoose and set her back on the ground, as did Death to Yoli. Rem still bade her to hold his hand, however, instructing her that he needed the touching.

A few moments later the group opened a door and took a winding staircase fashioned of hard clay to the floor below. Rem had said that the staircase led to the heart of the underground city.

Giselle stared in amazement at the dark underground world as she entered it, thinking it one of the neatest sights she'd ever clapped eyes on. It was full of music and laughter, pubs and trading stalls everywhere, homes dotted all around the city centre, all of the structures made of purple clay. The dark atmosphere was lightened up by constantly burning tiki torches, only instead of fire the torches seemed to be possessed of a neon-like gel substance.

The people of Joo were obviously a happy race as laughter and gaiety filled the air. It made Giselle smile. They were so carefree as to be enchanting.

The sounds of boasts and laughter drew the group's attention toward an auctioning block erected a few feet away. Giselle's smile faltered a bit when she realized that the objects being bartered off were women. Or to be more precise, potential brides.

"The next wench up for sale is the beautiful Fia," the auctioneer cried out while an extremely busty and very naked girl of no more than eighteen was led out onto the stage to a series of catcalls and whistles. "As you can see, Fia is possessed of exceptional beauty so her sire will accept only the grandest of bids. Do I hear a starting bid of fifty credits?"

Several hands flew up.

"Do I hear sixty? Seventy?..."

And so it went until it came down to two bidders, neither of them certain they wished to pay more than two hundred credits for the right to own Fia's beautiful silver body.

"Oh come now men!" the auctioneer cried, "what man amongst you wouldn't desire the right to rut in Fia's sweet channel every moon-rising?" He turned to the bride being auctioned off. "Fia, come sit before these gentlemen and show them your lusty cunt."

She complied with a smile, sitting down before the remaining two bidders and spreading her thighs wide.

"Show these men proper respect, wench," the auctioneer scolded her, "by spreading your cunt lips apart for their viewing pleasure."

Fia immediately did as she'd been told, murmuring an apology for not having done so to begin with.

For the next ten minutes the two bidders inspected every nuance of Fia's silver body. They licked at her labial folds, sucked on her clit until she came and they knew how she tasted, and tweaked and suckled on her distended nipples.

The girl next demonstrated why she was worth so many credits by sucking off both potential husbands to climax.

"And so you can see," the auctioneer continued, "that not only is Fia beautiful, but she is more than able to suckle her husband and her · husband's sire into happiness."

Giselle's lips pinched together disapprovingly. She supposed this wouldn't be the time most conducive to lecturing these people on the merits of the feminist movement—they needed their help to get off this planet after all—but the fact that the wives here were considered the sexual chattel of both the husband and the husband's father truly grated.

Sensing her mood, Rem looked down at his Sacred Mate and chuckled. "'Twill be but one moon-rising we stay here, my hearts. There is no need to get your spots in an uproar."

She shot him a withering look that spoke volumes, which only made him laugh all the harder. "Come," Rem said as he affectionately squeezed her hand, "let us go find a dining stall."

Giselle's stomach rumbled at the mere mention of food. "I hope their meals here are better than their manners toward women."

"Not really, but there is no other alternative left to us."

She could only groan.

Chapter 12
Two days later in Sand City...

Kil Q'an Tal, the King of Tryston's dominant red moon Morak, strode into the great hall of the Palace of the Dunes. He was greeted first by his nieces Zora and Zara, who bounded into his arms upon seeing him and dotted kisses all over his face.

"Did you bring us presents, uncle?" Zara asked excitedly.

"*Mani* said you made a stop in Galis a fortnight past," Zora added. "Did you bring us some of their candies?"

"Klea loved the holo-games you sent..."

"And Jun was bedeviled by..."

"Girls, girls," Kil said with an affectionate grin, "have you ever known your uncle to stop in Galis without bringing you back their wares?"

"Nay," Zora said placidly, quieter and more reserved than her twin by nature.

"This day is no different." He waved a hand toward one of his warriors. "Go collect your spoils from Jek."

Kil grinned as the twins bounded away then finished his stroll into the great hall. He stopped when he reached his brother's side and clapped him on the back. "I've come to celebrate Kara's come-out."

Zor turned around, surprised to see him here. "'Tis glad we are to have you with us and I know Kyra will be thrilled to see you again."

Kil nodded.

"But what do you here without Rem and his *nee'ka*?"

"I spoke to Rem last moon-rising. He and his bride are on Joo."

Zor teasingly waggled his eyebrows.

"Aye," Kil agreed, "they've the lustiest of wenches there." His lips kicked up into a semi-grin. "Though Rem has no care for them now."

Zor inclined his head, his expression solemn. "'Tis glad I am that Rem has found his true mate." He sighed as he ran a hand through his hair. "I cannot tell you how worried I've been after getting so many reports of his...devolution."

Kil clapped a hand around his brother's shoulder and led them to an area of the vast raised table where they could talk privately. "I've just left Ari," Kil confided as they took their seats.

"And? What did the Chief Priestess have to say?"

He waggled his eyebrows. "You mean besides the fact that I'm still the lustiest fuck on Tryston?"

Zor rolled his eyes. "Be serious dunce. Leastways," he sniffed, "Kyra will tell you 'tis your Emperor who holds that coveted title."

Kil did a little eye rolling of his own.

Zor grunted. "Just tell me what Ari said."

He nodded. "She proclaims that so long as Rem experiences no separations from his *nee'ka* he should be fully healed within a few Yessat years time." He spread his hands. "Her advice is for Giselle to milk his rod often, as well as for her to steer clear of consummation feasts until Rem is fully recovered."

"Hmm, it makes good sense."

"What is your meaning?"

Zor shrugged. "You are not mated, so you cannot understand yet. 'Tis difficult enough," he explained, "for a mated warrior to watch his *nee'ka* be fondled by other warriors without adding into the mix a biological ailment brought on by the cunning Jera." He shook his head. "The predator in all of us threatens to come out when a *nee'ka* is touched by another. But when the predator has been stirring beforehand..." He sighed. "'Tis dangerous to provoke it."

Kil chewed that over for a moment, his jaw clenching when he thought of — *her*. Of another warrior touching — *her*. Of that silky channel being offered up to a man other than himself.

He beleagueredly ran hand through his hair telling himself 'twas foolhardy to harbor such possessive feelings toward his recently acquired bound servant. Hadn't he taken a respite from Morak just to be away from her bedevilment? Hadn't he gone out seeking battles because she confused his emotions so sorely? Nay, he would not think on her.

"Leastways," Kil said, turning the subject, "Rem has assured me that he and his *nee'ka* fare well and that they are journeying towards the mountains of Joo to enter the seventh dimension through the holo-port there."

"Excellent."

"As you are aware the atmosphere of Joo makes it impossible to travel with a gastrolight cruiser beyond a certain point, so 'tis naught I can do to hurry along their journey. Leastways, I will still leave with a troop of my hunters after Kara's come-out to meet up with Rem near the mountains."

One dark eyebrow shot up. "Hunters? Why not take regular warrior guardsmen?"

Kil sighed. "I have not a care for the fact that the penal colony of Trukk lies in such close proximity to Joo." He shrugged. "I take my hunters merely as a precautionary measure."

Zor sniffed at that. "Warriors guard the portal that lies between the sixth and seventh dimensions. There is no reason to fear that a devolved creature might escape its asylum through the portal and travel into Joo."

"You mayhap have the right of it." He sighed. "But..."

"Aye?"

Kil shook his head. "The wenches on Joo are a lusty lot. What would happen, for instance, if the warrior guardsmen were lured to the *vesha* hides whilst a devolved creature broke loose from the penal colony? The creature could easily gain a portal into the sixth dimension and reek all sorts of blood-lust havoc."

"I think you see trouble where it doesn't exist, brother," Zor murmured.

"Mayhap," Kil agreed, "yet still will I feel better taking my hunters." He met his brother's gaze. "I never want Rem to behold the very creature he was nigh close to devolving into," he finished softly.

Zor nodded. "'Tis settled then." He glanced toward the other side of the great hall where Kyra was strolling towards their eldest hatchlings to give them good morn kisses. His *nee'ka's* jiggling breasts never failed to give him an instant erection. And because the women—and men for that matter—of Tryston don't age until a fortnight or so before their deaths, she was as beautiful as the day he'd claimed her over one hundred and eighty earth years ago. "If there is naught else to tell, I will go to my *nee'ka* and make certain all has been prepared for the feast on the morrow."

Kil's eyes lit up. "Ah!" he said, having almost forgotten his other news. "There is but one more thing."

"Aye?"

He grinned. "Rem's *nee'ka* has been milking his rod of life-force but three days and already she complains of the belly flutters to him."

Zor chuckled. "So we're to be uncles again, aye?"

"Aye."

"Excellent."

They were quiet for a moment and eventually Zor's thoughts turned back to the come-out. "Speaking of being uncles, our niece Jana will be here this moon-rising with Dak and Geris for Kara's come-out on the morrow. Kara, of course, is elated."

"'Twas just three weeks ago Jana had her own come-out."

"Aye." Zor grinned. "Kara is nigh unto bursting with excitement over the fact that she'll be permitted to don a *mazi* on the morrow. She was jealous when Jana got to sport one before her. Leastways you know how close those two have always been."

Kil nodded. "I bet Cam will mayhap be more excited about the *mazi* than even Kara is," he said wryly.

Zor chuckled. "For a certainty, brother."

Chapter 13

It took another full day of traveling by foot before the group of seven came to another purple clay door.

"Thank god!" Giselle wailed dramatically, pressing a palm to her forehead. "The further south we travel the hotter it gets." She winced when she glanced up at Rem's face, the perspiration dripping off of him so badly that he looked freshly showered.

Here she was complaining when he'd been thoughtful enough to carry her in the papoose the entire time. Of course, she thought dryly, it wasn't as if he hadn't gotten anything out of it. Once again she had been impaled on his cock the entire time, bringing him many an orgasm.

"We shall bed down for the night in the underground village, my hearts." He nodded to Death, telling him without words to open the door. "Let us just hope the inns below ground are more tempting than the ones we had to choose from in the last town."

Giselle could only agree. Harrumphing, she wrapped her arms about his neck after he fixed her *qi'ka* top so he could take her from the papoose. "I shudder to think what was making those scurrying sounds in our room last night."

Rem chuckled. "'Tis best if you don't ask."

Her hand slid through his as the group made their way through the purple clay door and descended the twisting staircase. Giselle breathed in the cool air with a smile and was happy to note that the city centre of this village looked a lot cleaner which probably meant that the sleeping establishments would also be cleaner.

Var pointed toward an elite looking inn a block down and the group set out to acquire their rooms. Giselle couldn't figure out why the silver and lavender men of this village were looking at her and Yoli so strangely as they walked passed, but they were to find out the answer to that question all too soon.

"I apologize my king, yet 'tis against the law for me to offer you accommodations unless the wenches of your traveling party comply with the dress code of the village." The lavender humanoid at the sleeping establishment's check-in chamber looked pointedly at Giselle and Yoli who in turn threw each other bewildered glances.

"Dress code?" Rem asked. "What sort of dress code have you here?"

"The women of Lii-Lii village are permitted no clothing at all, Your Majesty. Not even the noble wenches..."

Giselle's nostrils flared.

Bloody hell! As if a damned qi'ka *wasn't embarrassing enough!*

"Furthermore..."

She whimpered, wondering how much worse it would get.

"...'tis against the laws of Lii-Lii for a wench to roam about unattended."

Rem grunted. "What mean you by unattended?"

The inn master threw the women a haughty look. "They need to be leashed."

"Leashed?!" Giselle shrieked. "As in a dog collar with a leash?"

The inn master had no idea what a dog was so he pointed towards a couple walking by. Giselle's lips puckered into a frown as she visually confirmed that, indeed, the woman's male escort was leading her around by a dog collar and chain.

Bloody hell! Do the women here play fetch as well?!

Huffing, she crossed her arms over her breasts and glowered up at her husband. "I. Won't. Wear. That," she seethed, each word bit out through gritted teeth.

Rem did his best to hide his mirth—truly he did. Well sort of. "'Tis only for one moon-rising, my hearts." He waggled his eyebrows mischievously. "Mayhap you will develop a fondness for the leash and bring them into fashion in Trek Mi Q'an."

Her chin went up a notch. "I refuse to wear it," she sniffed.

A golden eyebrow shot up. "The closest village is a two-day trek from here. We all need sleep if, like in the last village, we are unable to barter for a hover-craft in Lii-Lii."

"I believe a new one goes up on the auctioning block on the morrow," the inn master droned on, "but I guarantee the tradesman will pay you no heed if your wenches cannot abide the law." He gentled his expression, taking pity upon Giselle for the first time. "I tell you this not to distress you, my Queen, but that you might realize the way of things here."

Giselle, however, was not moved by his small token of appeasement. "Forget it!" she fumed up to Rem, her nostrils flaring to wicked proportions. "I don't care if we have to walk every day for the next year, *I. Will. Not. Wear. That!*"

"You would make these warriors walk needlessly?" Rem asked softly, hoping to stir a sense of empathy and guilt in her.

"*Yes!*"

"*Nee'ka*," Rem scolded her in a chastising tone. He clucked his tongue and shook his head.

"Forget it," she ground out. Giselle's chin shot up resolutely, her back rigid, her stance unwavering. "I've put up with being kidnapped, I've even managed to overlook your growling and the occasional baring of fangs..." She went on to list every of Rem's alleged sins. "...but I will not, under any circumstances, endure the humiliation of wearing a damned collar and leash!"

"We've the need of a hover-craft so you will do my bidding." Rem's jaw clenched unforgivingly. "'Tis final, my word."

"Harrumph."

"Giselle," he barked, "remove your *qi'ka* anon and hand it to the inn master."

"No!"

"Have I the need to do it for you?" His eyes raked over her breasts. "I've my powers here, you do realize." He sighed, not wishing to force her hand if it could be helped. "'Tis for naught but one moon-rising," he reminded her in a reasonable tone.

"No!"

"Then you leave me no choice..."

"Rem don't! Please..."

Giselle pressed a hand to her forehead and closed her eyes. So much had happened to her this past week, so many changes, but this was by far the worst of them. The very symbolism of being leashed was degrading enough, but to know that he meant to see it through...

"Please show me some mercy," she whispered as she opened her eyes and pleaded with him.

Rem felt a pang of guilt stab his hearts but refused to be moved by it. Allied planet or no, it simply wasn't safe to spend months walking through the jungles and hilly terrain of Joo to accomplish what a hover-craft could do in a fortnight or so. They needed to reach that portal.

His eyes locked with hers. "No mercy," he murmured.

Giselle felt tears gathering in her eyes but she refused to give him the satisfaction of seeing them fall. "That seems to have been your motto ever since you stole me."

She turned away from her husband then, refusing to look at him. Drawing herself up to her full five feet and four inches, she regarded the inn master proudly as she removed her *qi'ka* and handed it to him. She ignored the sounds of the warriors around her sucking in their breath, realizing it was her uncovered freckles that had turned them on to such a great degree.

Bloody hell! They're all perverts!

The inn master accepted the women's clothing and stored it away for safe-keeping. That accomplished he strode over to Rem and handed him a collar and leash. Rem shook his head slightly indicating that if the deed had to be done then the man would have to see to it himself. Giselle, her back still turned to her husband, didn't witness his telling action.

The inn master sighed but relented. Standing before Giselle he was about to clasp the collar about her neck when his hands stilled. Her head shot up in time to watch the lavender man gulp and his silvery eyes bulge out of their sockets as his gaze swept over her naked body. "You are spotted," he whispered thickly, his erection instantaneous and highly noticeable.

Giselle rolled her eyes.

Bloody hell! Here we go again!

"'Tis *my* spots you covet," Rem ground out, his jaw clenching as his eyes flicked a warning green at the inn master. "I own them all." His hand made an angry slashing motion. "Clasp her if you must but be quick and be gone."

Giselle glared up at her husband as the collar was clasped unforgivingly about her neck just below her bridal necklace. Her nostrils flared as the attached leash was then handed over to Rem.

"Now then," the inn master carried on as though nothing untoward had just transpired, "let us get down to business, hm? The dining stalls are open until..."

Giselle listened with half an ear, not particularly caring if she ate tonight or not. She just wanted to go up to their suite. She just wanted to be away from her unbending husband and his total domination of her.

For the first time since this entire otherworldly ordeal began she found herself wanting to be as far away from Rem as was possible. She needed to be alone so she could think, so she could sort out her jumbled thoughts. Even one minute's worth of privacy would be considered a gift from the heavens.

As she ran her fingers through her hair in punishing strokes she wondered if she'd ever be able to forgive Rem for this last bit. Wasn't it bad enough that she'd been kidnapped from her home, refused the use of real clothing, and been made to endure his total possession of her? They'd crash landed onto a planet of translucent predators then ambled on over to a planet of misogynists. How much could she take?

"Bloody hell," Giselle whispered brokenly. "Bloody hell."

* * * * *

All throughout the evening repast Giselle refused to so much as make eye contact with Rem. He wasn't certain what he ought to do to remedy the situation, but his hearts were breaking as she continually rebuffed him.

Worse yet, he thought as his eyes narrowed menacingly, his *nee'ka* was quick to break bread and make jests with the other warriors — warriors who were forever ogling her bedeviling nipples and spots — but when it came to Rem she would make no concessions. He had told her she would be shown no mercy. Now 'twas his wee wife who had turned the tables on him.

The dining stall they were eating in was crudely fashioned but elegant enough. Rather than tables and benches, each party was given a *vesha* pad to lounge upon on the floor where everyone reclined on their elbows and fed from platters of meat, bread, and berries. The chamber was lit up by gel-lamps contained within wall sconces, giving the place a decidedly erotic air about it.

Apparently Rem wasn't the only male humanoid who felt that way for a quick glance around the chamber to the other *vesha* pads showed males coupling with their leashed women everywhere in sight. Even Death and Yoli were playing with each other, Yoli purring as Death buried his face between her legs and suckled her clit into climax.

When Rem could endure no more separation he made a shooing motion toward his warriors in such a way that Giselle could not see it. They grinned and obliged, making their excuses to the Queen that 'twas time for them to roam up to the *matpow* bar across the chamber that they might find a bit of bedsport with the wenches drinking there.

When they were gone from the *vesha* pad Rem telekinetically summoned off his warrior's garb and scooted closer to his *nee'ka*, unsubtly pressing his erection against her backside as he ran a large hand over her reclining form.

Giselle's back stiffened as they laid on their sides, her back to his front. "I'm not in the mood," she said quietly.

Rem palmed one of her breasts, the pad of his thumb circling her distended nipple as he laved at her ear with his tongue. "Do not hold a grudge against me, my hearts," he murmured. "We will burn the wretched collar the moment we leave Lii-Lii. You've my word."

She softened a bit at that caring proclamation, but wasn't quite ready to let bygones be bygones. "It frightens me," she admitted on a whisper, "that you are so unyielding where I am concerned."

Rem's entire body stilled. "I cannot believe you see it that way." He plucked a nipple as he sighed. "I am bedeviled by you for a certainty. I am but moldable *trelli* sand in your hands."

She couldn't suppress the tiny smile that found its way to her lips. "Then why is everything always your way or no way?" she asked seriously.

He thought that over for a protracted moment. "I suppose 'tis true it appears that way just now..." He ran his hand over her belly, the belly she didn't yet realize was carrying his hatchling. "...but ever since I claimed you there has been naught but life-threatening circumstance after life-threatening circumstance. I cannot take chances with your safety, my hearts, nor can I take chances," he murmured, "with the life of our unborn *pani*."

Pani? Didn't that mean—

Giselle felt as though the breath had been knocked out of her. Her head darted up to glance over her shoulder and meet Rem's glowing blue gaze. "A child?" she whispered. "I'm pregnant?"

He gently nudged her onto her back and settled himself between her thighs. Craning his neck, he bent it to sweetly kiss her lips and dart his tongue into her mouth.

He made a few soft brushstrokes then raised his head to meet her rounded eyes. With much emotion in his expression, he nodded. "Aye," he shakily confirmed.

"Oh my god," she breathed out. Her eyes locking with his, she felt his every emotion, felt the pain and the torture of having longed for hundreds of years for a child, felt the agony of having believed himself to be forever damned to a life without a true mate and offspring. Hundreds of years worth of grief mingled with a tiny spark of hope borne but four nights past was so overwhelming to Giselle that unshed tears burned in the backs of her eyes for him. "Oh Rem."

In that moment she wanted to be joined to his body more fiercely than she could ever remember having wanted something in the past. With a strength she didn't even know she possessed, she rolled her surprised Sacred Mate onto his back, straddled his lap, and plunged her flesh downwards to impale herself on his cock.

"*Nee'ka*," he said hoarsely, his large hands reaching up to palm her buttocks, "does this mean you have forgiven your Sacred Mate?"

She groaned out her yes as she sank down onto him, finding a pace that heightened their mutual pleasure. "I love you," she whispered as she locked eyes with him, "and I can't wait to have your baby."

"My hearts," he murmured, running his hands over her breasts and massaging her nipples while she rode him, "I love you more than 'tis possible to express with mere words."

Giselle closed her eyes briefly as if savoring the moment. She, a woman who had been a spinster but a week ago, had never thought to have this intimate bond with a man. Rem wasn't the only one who knew a thing or two about loneliness. She realized it was but a drop in the hat compared to what he had experienced, but back on earth she could have written the book on the subject.

"Prove it," she said with a coy expression as she bent over him and rode him so that her breasts were dangling in his face, "suck on my *migi*-candies."

She was teasing him, he knew, wanting them to dwell on the pleasure of the present, the glory of the future, rather than on the grief of the past.

He grinned. "'Tis my favorite treat."

Giselle half chuckled and half groaned as he popped a nipple into his mouth and suckled from it. Within mere moments she needed to climax so badly that she had to sit back up so she was seated fully on his thick erection. Her breasts jiggled wantonly as she closed her eyes and rode him hard.

"Mmm," Rem purred, his hands reaching behind her to knead her buttocks, "'tis the sweetest channel in the goddess' creation."

"Oh Rem."

Giselle's breathing grew labored as she impaled herself on his shaft, her flesh suctioning in his as their bodies mated. "I love your cock," she admitted breathlessly, "it's so thick and filling."

"'Tis yours," he ground out, "all yours."

Rem's need to dominate her body took over, inducing him to roll her onto her back and slide into her flesh in a series of long, quick thrusts. Grabbing one of her thighs, he nudged it upwards and burrowed into her channel to the hilt.

"Oh god."

"Tell me what you want," he arrogantly commanded her. He rotated his hips and slammed into her fast and deep. *"Tell me."*

"You," Giselle groaned. She wrapped her legs around his hips and held on for a hard ride. *"I want your cum."*

He picked up the pace of his thrusting. "'Tis my life-force you covet?" he ground out, his jaw clenched tightly.

"Oh god yes."

"Then milk my rod, *nee'ka.*"

Giselle's head fell back on a moan. His thrusting was driving her toward delirium, the feel of him burrowing into her flesh exquisite. Within seconds she was shouting out a hoarse cry, an intense orgasm ripping through her belly. Her nipples stabbed upwards as blood rushed up to heat her face and her vagina convulsed around Rem's cock.

He joined her in bliss but a fraction of a moment later, the spurting of his seed inducing the bridal necklace to pulse. They held onto each other and moaned, their bodies trembling and convulsing with a euphoric mutual hedonism.

When the waves of peaking had passed and their breathing began to steady they remembered for the first time that they had coupled in a filled dining stall. From Death and Yoli, to Rem's warriors, to the citizens of Lii-Lii, they could only chuckle at the wide-eyed looks everyone was throwing them.

Giselle grinned up at Rem and wrapped her arms about his neck. The former spinster felt like a vixen and she loved him all the more for it.

Chapter 14
Meanwhile in Sand City...

The High Princess Kara Q'ana Tal paced within her royal apartments as she anxiously awaited the arrival of her best friend and cousin, Princess Jana Q'ana Tal. Jana had set out for the great hall on a mission and now Kara could do naught but wait for her return.

Kara's teeth sank into her bottom lip as she continued to pace. When the doors to her chamber flew open a few minutes later and the beautiful golden Jana strode in, Kara flew across the room and grabbed a hold of her shoulders. "Well," she whispered, her glowing blue eyes rounded, "what does he look like?"

Jana grinned, deciding to toy with her a bit. She shrugged out of Kara's hold and sauntered over to the raised bed. "Are you sure you want to know?" she threw over her shoulder, her expression coy.

"For a certainty."

Jana giggled, giving up her game. "Oh Kara, he is the handsomest of warriors," she said with the drama only a girl of eighteen can perfect. She took Kara's hands in her own as they sank down onto the raised bed to gossip. "He's as tall and thickly muscled as our sires and fair-haired like mine..."

Kara's breath caught in her throat.

"...his eyes are the most beautiful shade of glowing turquoise-green I've ever beheld. In truth, they've the same color as the most vintage bottle of *matpow*."

"And?" Kara asked excitedly, "what of his cock?"

Jana nodded, grinning. "'Tis an ominous bulge your future Sacred Mate carries about in his leathers."

Kara admittedly knew next to nothing about shafts and man sacs, but she'd often heard her *mani* praise her papa over his lusty thick cock. 'Twas best if big, she could only conclude. "Which *mazi* should I wear do you think?"

"Hmm," Jana murmured, tapping a finger against her cheek. "Mayhap the blue to show your respect." She nodded definitively. "'Tis the emblem of High Lords and 'twill match the color of your betrothed's leathers. Besides," she shrugged, "it matches your eyes and goes well against your lovely black hair."

"You've a point with the last bit," Kara conceded. She threw her an impish grin. "But what of the other bit? Do I really want to appear as though I am all things submissive and complacent right from the start? Leastways he'll be bored of me outside of two Nuba-minutes if I do that." Her eyebrows rose fractionally. "Especially considering the fact my family would know it to be a lie."

Jana giggled. "So bedevil him then."

"Oh? And how do I do that?"

"Well," she said in a worldly tone, feeling vastly more knowledgeable on the subject of warriors since she'd been permitted to dine with them for three full weeks now, "wear the blue *mazi* to show your respect but flirt with the other warriors." She wagged an instructional finger. "Never let him think that you're his for the taking."

Kara frowned at that. "I am his for the taking," she said quietly, not sure how she felt about the fact that she'd never know a day of freedom before being claimed. "Leastways now that I am eighteen 'tis understood by all and sundry that he owns me by the Holy Law." She shook her head, her voice lowering to a threadbare whisper. "*Mani* and papa are but figureheads now, two people my betrothed entrusts to keep my channel virgin until he claims me in seven Yessat years."

Jana sighed, squeezing her hand to remind her of her support. "'Tis true, your words."

Kara took a calming breath. "What if I hate him, Jana?" she whispered. "What if the goddess seeks to punish me for past transgressions by giving me into the care of a beast?"

Jana felt Kara's anguish as if it were her own. "Then we will shall flee this galaxy forever...together."

Kara's head shot up. She sucked in her breath. "Do you mean that?"

Jana nodded definitively. "'Tis a vow amongst best friends."

Kara swiped at the tears falling from her eyes. She searched Jana's gaze. "Best friends forever?" she murmured.

"Aye." Jana threw her arms around her and they embraced with the fierce and untainted passion of eighteen-year-old girls. "Best friends forever."

* * * * *

High Lord Cam K'al Ra had never felt so nervous in all of his Yessat years. He had spent the morn of this day fantasizing about what Kara might look like, then spent the afternoon working out his anxiousness and lust on a bevy of bound servants and *Kefas*. He had had his needs seen to as the Emperor had instructed him, yet still he felt no surcease.

Upon entering the great hall, he saw that all had taken their seats and were assembled around the vast raised table awaiting the moment when his future Sacred Mate would make her appearance on her sire's arm and the feasting would begin. Tons and tons of presents were lined up on another table, all of them come-out gifts for the High Princess Kara.

Cam strode toward the empty seat next to Klea, the High Princess who was to have her come-out in a few months. Still in the *kazi*, his seventeen-year-old future sister-within-the-law reveled in the moment of being able to dine amongst the assembled warriors, for 'twas only upon celebratory occasions a girl-child could do so before her come-out.

On the right of Klea sat the High King Jor. The Emperor's heir continually threw glares at the warriors who dared look upon Klea over long. Cam noted that the High King was filling out rapidly, having already developed a heavier musculature since he'd dined with him last moon-rising.

On the other side of Jor sat wee Geris, the seven-year-old High Princess who had been named for the Empress' best friend and sister-within-the-law, the Queen of the green moon Ti Q'won. Like Zora and Zara, who were seated next to their youngest sister, wee Geris sported the same fire-berry locks as their *mani*, Kara and Klea being the only two daughters who had inherited their sire's black hair.

The only of the ruling family Cam noticed was absent was two-year-old Jun, the King of planet Zolak. Cam noted the hour, realizing 'twas no doubt past the wee King's bedtime.

Plopping down into his seat next to Klea, Cam took note of the fact that the Empress was seated to his left. She hadn't noticed his arrival just yet though, for she was embroiled in a heated discussion with the couple seated to her left, Queen Geris and King Dak. 'Twas because of the fact he'd taken his seat with the Empress unawares that

Cam overheard a conversation he had likely been meant never to be made privy to.

"I'm not certain what to do about Kara." Kyra shook her head and sighed. "How is Dari dealing with it, Ger?"

Geris did a little sighing of her own as she glanced first to her husband and then to her best friend. "Not well at all."

"What's this?" Dak asked, clearly astounded by his wife's confession. "'Tis the first I've heard that my daughter is troubled."

Kyra glanced across the raised table to where the fourteen-year-old Princess Dari was seated next to a few of her siblings. Where most of Geris and Dak's six children favored their father with his golden hair and golden skin, Dari and her three-year-old sister Hera were the spitting images of Geris, their long black locks plaited away from their faces in micro-braids that hung to their waists, their dark African-inherited skins a deep onyx. On this planet, as in all of Trek Mi Q'an galaxy, Dari and Hera were considered highly coveted marriage prizes for their rare skins alone. And all of Geris and Dak's children, Dari and Hera included, were possessed of the ever-sought-after glowing blue eyes of the Q'an Tal bloodline.

"I don't think the warriors here take into consideration the way a young girl feels when she knows her life has already been chosen for her," Geris explained to her husband, her lips puckering into the trademark frown she used when agitated with her Sacred Mate.

Dak harrumphed. "You best explain yourself, *nee'ka*."

Geris sighed as if the answer should have been obvious. "Dari knows that she will never get to experience a moment of freedom, that she will never get to do all of the fun things most Trystonni girls get to do when they reach the age of twenty-five and legally become women."

She shook her head. "We both know that Gio will take her away the very moment she comes into the claimable age."

Dak's eyes narrowed. "I have not a care for the way you say our future son-within-the-law's name, *nee'ka*. 'Tis true Gio was a bit of a ne'er-do-well in his youth, but he has grown into the finest of warriors. Indeed," he plowed on, "he might have inherited the title of High Lord from his sire rather than having earned it, but 'tis whispered about that Zor will give unto Gio another sector as reward for his hunting prowess." He spread his hands in a gesture of pride. "I cannot name a warrior more worthy of my beloved Dari's hand."

Geris huffed, her arms crossing under her engorged breasts. "As usual, you have totally missed my point. I suspect you do it on purpose!"

"Do not backtalk me, *nee'ka*," he sniffed in a kingly tone, "else will you be grounded from your woman's joy yet again."

Her lips pinched together in a glower. "I might have fallen for that line seventeen Yessat years ago, but that threat is useless now."

"Oh? How so?"

"Because you can't take the separation," she murmured. Geris ran her tongue seductively about her upper lip while she meaningfully fingered her bridal necklace. She watched her Sacred Mate gulp roughly. "Grounding me grounds you as well."

Dak's jaw tightened. "You best stop toying with me, *nee'ka*," he ground out, "else will I sample of your charms at this very table."

"The point is," Kyra smoothly interjected before Dak lost his control and began mating with Geris right in front of her, "that Kara and Dari are both feeling as though they have been cheated of the rite of passage most females here take for granted that they'll have." She shook her head. "Trek Mi Q'an is a vast galaxy of warriors with very few female hatchings. I've only lived here eighteen Yessat years and even I know that most females here realize they will have a period of freedom in between reaching adulthood and being claimed for the sole reason that the chances of them having bumped into their Sacred Mates in such a huge galaxy before they experience a time of freedom is rare." She shrugged. "Kara and Dari are two of only a handful of exceptions I can think of."

Dak begrudgingly conceded to that fact. "I take your meaning," he muttered.

Cam felt his entire body stiffen even as his heart rates accelerated and his nostrils flared in possessiveness. Every day without Kara felt an eternity. He, who was over twice his betrothed's age, would not be able to wait even a Nuba-second once she reached five and twenty and he could legally sample of her charms. He would care for his *pani* bride well and love her with all of his hearts, but she would be given no reprieve. 'Twas final, his decision.

Realistically Cam knew that he now owned Kara and that she would therefore have no say in the matter of being claimed, but he couldn't suppress the worry he felt that the Empress might seek to intervene on his betrothed's behalf and somehow thwart the claiming. He would have to speak on this matter to the Emperor later, warrior to warrior.

"I know Gio is a fine warrior as is Cam," Kyra said gently to Dak, "I don't take issue with that fact. I'm merely trying to point out what Kara and Dari are going through because I have no idea how to deal with it."

Cam felt his body relax. Mayhap he would not need to speak with the Emperor after all. Mayhap all he needed to do was speak with the Empress in privacy later to reassure her he would make for a fine Sacred Mate. The High Princess Kara might harbor her doubts now, but 'twas for a certainty she would be fine once he joined her to him for all times.

Cam felt a pang of empathy for Gio when he watched the High Lord take a seat next to the exquisitely beautiful Dari only to be rebuffed by his future bride. The Princess, who was allowed in Gio's presence only because 'twas a celebratory occasion, refused to speak with him, turning her attention instead toward her golden elder sister Jana. Cam could almost hear Gio's teeth grinding together from his own seat.

"Cam," the Empress said worriedly, finally taking note of his presence, "how long have you been sitting there?"

When he turned to Kyra he saw that she was nibbling on her lower lip. "Long enough," he murmured.

"Oh Cam." The Empress placed her hand atop his and squeezed. "Kara will come around eventually. I know she will."

He wasn't given any time to respond to that assertion for the guest of honor and her sire strode into the great hall just then, stopping at the head of the table where Kara would sit with the Emperor throughout the feast.

Cam sucked in his breath, the beauty of his betrothed's visage carrying the same impact as a telekinetic punch in the abdomen. "By the goddess," he murmured, his eyes hungrily raking in every nuance of her fertile form.

Kara was dressed in a blue *mazi*, the skirt shielding her mons from his gaze but the split up the left side showing off her creamy golden skin clear to the hip. The strapless bikini-like top she wore was completely see-through and afforded him an unimpeded view of large breasts capped off with long, thick nipples.

The High Princess' dark hair had been left in all its unbound glory, cascading down her back in black ringlets all the way to her buttocks. And when her gaze found his and she nervously chewed on her bottom lip Cam confirmed that her eyes were the same mesmerizing glowing blue they had been when last he'd seen her. His erection was so fast and rigid that it broached painful.

Kara, her hand in her father's, smiled up at her sire as he proudly announced her to the feasting party. "Warriors and wenches, I give you my third-born and beloved daughter, the High Princess Kara Q'ana Tal." He grinned at the warriors' murmurs of approval. "A bedeviling beauty she is, but 'tis best if the lot of you remember that High Lord Cam K'al Ra owns her as of this moon-rising."

Cam lounged on his bench arrogantly, thankful to the Emperor for reinforcing his status before all and sundry.

"Cam," the Emperor said in formal, ceremonial tones, "My *nee'ka* and I thank-you for entrusting us with the care of your betrothed until she reaches the claimable age and we both do vow to deliver Kara unto you with a virgin channel on her twenty-fifth birthday."

Cam nodded his gratitude but said nothing.

"Come," the Emperor commanded him, "and dine next to your future Sacred Mate."

Chapter 15

*The portal separating the sixth
and seventh dimensions, two weeks later...*

Kil's hand fisted in cold fury as he took in the sight around him. His worst nightmare, the very one Zor had called him fanciful for even dreaming up, had come to pass.

A devolved creature had escaped the penal colony within the seventh dimension and massacred everything it came across thereafter. The warrior guardsmen, too preoccupied with plunging their rods into the channels of the lusty Joo wenches, had been taken unawares, the result being that all of them were now dead, what was left of their carcasses already dined upon.

Having been offered no resistance, the creature had made its way through the portal and into the sixth dimension where even now it would be on the hunt for more humanoid blood. A devolved creature was insatiable in its hunger, a predator that needed flesh and blood to sustain it.

Kil considered the timing of this fiasco and had not a care for it. Rem and Giselle should be nearing Mount Lia any day now, Mount Lia being the last natural barrier between Joo and the portal.

Worse yet, he conceded, Giselle was due to hatch at any time now. Kil closed his eyes briefly as he recalled the excitement in Rem's voice upon telling him through a holographic communication of Giselle's pregnancy. When the hatching came his youngest brother would be too overwhelmed with emotion to take note of anything save his *nee'ka* and their emerging *pani* sac.

Kil opened his eyes and ran a punishing hand through his hair. He could only hope that he and his hunters would be able to intercept the blood-hungry creature before it took out his family unawares. And if not, he could only hope that the creature didn't track down their scents during the few hours time it would take for Giselle to finish hatching. 'Twas the only time, he knew, when a warrior so strong as Rem could be taken unawares.

* * * * *

From the foot of Mount Lia, Giselle gawked up at the huge natural barrier separating their party of seven from the portal which would take them to Rem's home dimension and galaxy. "Are you certain the hover-craft can't make it up there?" she asked, her hand automatically flying to her flat belly to rub it when she felt a fluttering inside of it.

"Aye, 'tis for a certainty," Rem confirmed, his eyes raking over her naked form. Giselle had had to leave her *qi'ka* back in the village of Lii-Lii because the hover-craft tradesman would do no business with them otherwise. For the past fortnight her body had been completely bared to his inspection and he never got tired of the sight of it.

Unfortunately, he conceded with down-turned lips, neither did his warriors. Her spots and lush form bedeviled the lot of them, all of the warriors having found themselves in need of frequent stops to find a willing channel to rut into after lusting over her charms for a spell.

"You will not have to walk," Rem promised her in a voice thick with desire, "I will put you in your papoose."

Giselle's lips pinched together as she threw her husband an exasperated look. "This will be a lot of walking!" she pointed out. "Do you really think it's a good idea to expend so much extra energy?"

"'Tis invigorating to be milked by you, my hearts."

"We just finished doing it five minutes ago," she sniffed, "you can't possibly be ready to do it again, let alone do it while you walk up a mountain!"

He ran his fingers through her thatch of strawberry-blonde curls, his thumb easily honing in on her clit. Her eyes immediately glazed over. "You know I cannot stand to be separated from this channel," he murmured. "I need your flesh wrapped about me, milking me always." He rubbed her clit more briskly. "We will not be able to couple for a full fortnight once you hatch, *nee'ka*. 'Twill like as not be the death of me," he finished hoarsely.

Giselle's breath caught in her throat as an orgasm began building. A fortnight did sound like an unbearable amount of time. Nevertheless, she didn't want her husband to think she was a milksop unable to deny him anything. Begin as you mean to go on, she'd always said. Then again, she conceded on a moan when his other hand began toying with her nipples, a little papoose time had never hurt anybody.

Bloody hell! She was the milkiest of milksops!

"Oh alright," she grandly declared in her best martyr's voice, her hand flying dramatically to her brow, "I suppose it's best for the baby if you carry us."

Rem suppressed a chuckle as he took Giselle's hand and led her towards the hover-craft where the papoose was being stored. "'Tis a thoughtful *mani* you are."

She threw him a scowl, knowing he was humoring her. "If you think I'll always do your bidding merely because you can do that bridal necklace thing, then think again."

He grunted as he began securing the harness to himself. "Have I told you yet how a Trystonni warrior punishes a recalcitrant Sacred Mate?"

She crossed her arms under her breasts and thrust her chin up regally. "How?"

Rem plucked her up off of the purple clay ground, slipped her legs through the harness, and impaled her in one fluid motion. "We ground them from their woman's joy."

"How wicked," she breathed out.

Giselle sucked in her breath and moaned as her husband began to walk. She knew her buttocks were bared to anyone who should pass behind her which made what they were doing all the more erotic.

An hour and multiple orgasms later, she knew Rem was toying with her, grounding her as it was from the ultimate woman's joy. He still hadn't released his life-force which her body was frenziedly trying to milk from him in a series of intense climaxes. Every time she came he gritted his teeth as her vagina convulsed, then grinned down at her when he'd regained control of himself.

Her nostrils flaring, she decided she'd had enough. If her bridal necklace didn't pulse soon she was likely to go mad.

"Oh Rem," Giselle breathed out seductively, her eyes closing as she used her hands to massage her own nipples, "I'd give anything for your cum."

He gulped — roughly.

She went in for the kill, running her fingers tantalizingly across the splash of light freckles over her cleavage. She could see his jaw clenching. "When you come inside of me," she said in a throaty murmur, "it makes my spots tingle like—"

His fingers dug into the flesh of her hips and he surged upwards on a hoarse shout of sexual release. The bridal necklace pulsated so rapidly that their mutual cries could be heard throughout the mountain.

When it was over and the wave of sexual peaks had ceased, it was Giselle who was doing the grinning this time. Begin as you mean to go on, she'd always said.

* * * * *

That night around a gel-based campfire, Giselle laid on her stomach atop a *vesha* hide and watched through glazed-over eyes as the warriors in their entourage found their pleasure with a gorgeous lavender woman who had traveled by foot for two days just to have sex with the lusty warriors.

The group of seven had made camp this evening in the midst of the jungle for they hadn't come across another purple clay door while trekking today. That was just as well to Giselle's way of thinking for every time they stopped in a new village the customs concerning the lot in life for the women within them had grown increasingly appalling.

In the village of Lii-Lii, women weren't permitted the use of clothing and had to be leashed. In the village of Cunt—it had really been named that!—women not only had to be naked and leashed, but whenever they spoke with a male they had to show him the "proper respect" due to his gender by keeping their thighs spread wide and their vaginal lips opened for the males to lust over while they did so.

Giselle remembered the embarrassment she had suffered through when their group had dined out the night they had stayed in Cunt—she had had to keep her legs spread wide open the entire time for any man to gaze upon while Rem had hand-fed her the meal. And indeed, the men of the village had been more than happy to ogle her exposed flesh, many of them stopping at their purple clay table to clap Rem on the back and congratulate him on the capture of a bride with spots. Rather than getting angry Rem had puffed up with pride, his arrogance a tangible thing. She still gritted her teeth whenever she thought back on how he'd then proceeded to point out some of his favored spot formations, such as the Little Dipper on the swell of her bosom.

Bloody hell! She felt like an exotic zoo creature!

But nothing, she conceded, could have prepared her for the total misogyny they had found in the village of Treeka. Giselle sighed, remembering that sordid city centre all too well for they'd just left it behind two days past.

In Treeka the single women of the village were disallowed the use of credits and as a consequence had to barter for their wares with sucklings. Everywhere one went within Treeka the sight of lavender and silver women on their knees paying homage to an erect cock could be readily seen. The male would close his eyes in rapture while a female attended to him, burst in her mouth when he could endure no more stimulation, pat her on the head or perhaps squeeze a nipple, then send her on her way with the bartered wares.

If a woman was particularly good at suckling, the male she was bartering with had the legal right to claim her as a bride and add her into his own harem of wives. Giselle still remembered how guards had squired one young woman away after she'd given a tradesman the suckling of his life. The tradesman had bade her to be prepared for his thrusts when he returned home that moon-rising then had commanded his men to whisk her off. He had then gone on to sample of the temptations the next single females in line had to offer him.

The lavender woman attending even now to the warriors across the campfire heralded from Treeka, Giselle knew. She'd seen the busty girl getting it on with Rem's men while they were there, apparently quite loving the feel of so many virile cocks hardened and thrusting into her every crevice.

She supposed, Giselle admitted to herself, that she couldn't fault the lavender beauty for that. These warriors were all handsome of face and thickly muscled of form...no doubt an erotic dream come true for a single female not yet placed within a harem.

"Mmm, Tya," Var murmured as he gritted his teeth and slid into her flesh from behind, "you've a talented cunt, my lovely."

She giggled, enjoying the compliment, then groaned as his thrusts became lustier. Turned on, she reveled in Var's mating while snuggling her face into another warrior's lap and suckling his erect rod. The warrior groaned, his large fingers running through her hair as she attended to him.

The third warrior was sprawled out on a *vesha* hide near the gel-fire, already asleep and snoring quite loudly, the talented Tya having previously attended to his needs a few times.

At first Giselle had been a little disconcerted by the lusty play happening just a gel-fire away, the scene being one a woman rarely saw back on earth unless she had watched it in a porn film. But after an hour or so of watching the ever-ready Tya work her impressive wiles on the warriors, she had gotten used to the scene and had eventually been turned on by it.

So when Rem joined Giselle on the *vesha* hide and slid into her from behind, her flesh was already wet and welcoming.

"Ah *nee'ka*," he murmured, his voice whisper-soft, "I've missed this sweet channel sorely."

She closed her eyes on a moan, a small smile tugging at her lips. "You just had me an hour or two ago."

He rotated his hips and went deeper causing her to suck in her breath. "Far too long," he said thickly. "'Twould be a gift from the goddess Aparna did you submit to my lust every moment of every day."

"Rather than every other moment, you mean?"

He grinned, sliding into her fully, moving his hips about until she came. "Aye." He sat up when her body finished convulsing, drew her up to her knees on all fours, and pounded into her from behind. Reaching below her body, his hands found her breasts and plucked at her nipples. "Gis," he ground out, "I would that I could live within this channel at all times."

"Rem."

Giselle arched her back and groaned as his mating grew wilder. He impaled her in long, deep, rapid thrusts, hitting the sensitive spot within her vagina every time. *"Oh god."*

"Do you like that?" Rem arrogantly asked her through a clenched jaw. He continued to plump her nipples as he rode her flesh hard.

"I love it."

"You have not milked me enough to be rewarded with life-force just yet." He picked up the pace of his thrusting, impaling her rapidly as his fingers dug into the flesh of her hips. "Let me feel your woman's joy again."

"Oh — Rem." Giselle came for him again, her nipples stabbing out as she did so. She moaned like a wanton,

wanting more of his cock, wanting him to give her more pleasure. Thrusting her hips back at him, she gloried in the sound of his groans as she met each of his impalements with an equally lusty thrust. She could hear his flesh slapping into hers, feel the fingers that dug into her hips in their passion.

"'Tis *my* channel," he gritted out as he pounded into her mercilessly. "'Tis lucky you are when I claimed you that you carried not the scent of a primitive male." He clutched her hips tightly, the muscle in his jaw flexing as he prepared to spurt inside of her. "I would have tracked down the male the scent belonged to and..."

"*Oh god.*" She interrupted him on a groan, her flesh convulsing around his as she came. Her face felt like it was on fire it was so hot from the rush of blood the orgasm brought her.

Rem slammed into her body three times more then, unable to keep from bursting a moment longer, bellowed out his satisfaction on a hoarse cry as he drove into her channel fully and erupted into the mouth of her womb.

Giselle's eyes rolled back into her head as the bridal necklace began to pulse, her screams loud enough to be heard for miles away. She rode out the never-ending waves of pleasure, basking in each and every one of them until her body went numb.

Several minutes later when her body was cooled down enough to sleep, she climbed up onto her husband's massive torso and purred while he rubbed her buttocks. Smiling, she dotted little kisses all over his chest.

Bloody hell! She loved her bridal necklace!

Chapter 16
Meanwhile in Sand City...

The High Princess Kara selected her white *mazi* to wear for the first private meeting she was to have with her future Sacred Mate. Cam had unexpectedly had to leave immediately following her come-out due to some trouble in his sector and she hadn't heard heads or tails from him since.

Not that she had cared, she reminded herself. She didn't know how to go about dealing with a betrothed she wasn't altogether certain that she wanted—or would ever want. He was handsome, aye, but then so was freedom to a girl who had lived a sheltered existence all of her life.

Whilst she knew in her hearts that 'twas best to grow accustomed to the idea of being claimed in seven Yessat years, her mind kept screaming out a need for choice and freedom. She wanted to tool about Galis with Jana, the deuce of them spending all manner of credits at the shopping stalls by day then staying up until all hours of the moon-rising flirting with warriors. She wanted to do all of the things most females got to do when they reached the age of five and twenty, the things her other sisters and female cousins would get to do one day.

But nay, she thought with a sigh, like Dari the course of her existence had already been mapped out. All of her life Kara had been groomed for her future role as Cam K'al Ra's Sacred Mate just as Dari was perpetually being prepared to be claimed by Gio.

There was no alternative left to Kara today but to deal with Cam, she mentally conceded as she left her apartments and strode down the corridor that led to her brother Jor's rooms. She wanted to speak with the brother she'd always been so close to before the hour of reprieve was up and she would be forced by politesse to answer Cam's summons. She supposed she could refuse to see him, but like as not her sire would go in a rage if she did so and command her to speak with her betrothed any way. What was the point in refusing him? she sighed.

When Kara reached Jor's rooms the doors were opened by a bound servant whose puffy red lips looked as though they'd recently been suckling something. She wondered why a bound servant was answering her brother's chambers to begin with when he wasn't slated to gain a harem until a sennight hence.

Upon entering his bedchamber, she had her answer. "Oh of course," she mumbled to herself as her eyes raked the chamber and took note of all the naked bound servants lined up, awaiting their turn to pleasure her brother with their hands and mouths. Kara had forgotten that Jor was to choose the members of his harem this moon-rising that they might be assembled and awaiting his lust upon his birthday.

Kara was happy for Jor in that he was to be gifted with his harem next week. Unlike their *mani* who for inexplicable reasons balked at discussing sexual things with her sons, Kara had spoken with her brother many times concerning his needs and he had confided to her that 'twas naught but torture to be kept from spilling his life-force in a tight channel. She didn't want Jor in physical pain, so she thought 'twas wondrous he would have fifty tight channels awaiting him in a mere sennight's time.

Kara felt guilty disturbing him as her eyes flicked to the raised bed and she noted the look of bliss upon her brother's face. His eyes were closed as his head was pillowed by a massive pair of breasts that were attached to the distended nipples he took turns suckling of. Another bound servant was showing Jor her skill for shaft-suckling in the hopes of being chosen by him whilst another attended to his man sac with the same hope in mind.

It still struck Kara as curious the way her brother had grown into manhood this past fortnight. His voice had totally deepened, his musculature was thick and heavy, and his height had shot up to almost eight feet, surpassing the heights of even their sire and uncles.

She supposed a warrior so massive must have a lot of life-force to spurt. She decided not to disturb him from his pleasures and opted instead to sneak out unseen from his chambers. She supposed she could always seek Jor out later, after she'd met with her betrothed — and if he wasn't still busy choosing which of the wenches would be given the privilege of attending to him until he bored of them.

Kara took a deep breath and resigned herself to her fate. Her future Sacred Mate had bade her to appear before him and he owned her by the Holy Law. What choice did she have but to go to him?

Indeed, she thought angrily, she had no choice at all.

* * * * *

Although the *Kefas* had seen to his needs but a few minutes past, Cam's cock sprung immediately to life the moment wee Kara strode into his bedchamber wearing a white *mazi*. The top she wore was completely transparent and her thick nipples were stabbing up against the material. He'd never seen nipples so long and hard as hers and it filled him with an arrogant pride that they belonged to him alone.

He could tell that she was a bit nervous about being alone without escort in the same chamber as a naked, bathing man not of her relation. But she belonged to him now and because she did he thought it prudent to spend the next seven Yessat years preparing her for his lust.

"You summoned me, my lord?" she asked quietly, her glowing blue eyes flicking warily about.

Cam stood up and strode from the waters, his huge erection there for her to see. He heard a small sound as if she'd sucked in her breath before she skittishly darted her eyes away from his manhood. He quickly dried himself off, then took a seat on a *vesha* bench, his back supported by the whisper-soft throne-like chair. "'Tis glad I am to at last be alone with you," he murmured.

She nodded but said nothing.

"Will you not remove your *mazi* for me," he said thickly, "and come sit upon my lap?"

Kara's head shot up. She eyed his rampant erection with a mix of trepidation and curiosity. She knew 'twas his right to touch her as he desired so long as he didn't join with her. Still, rights or no rights, she didn't know this man, hadn't spend time with him in over five Yessat years, and no longer knew if she could trust him. "I-I thought," she stammered out dumbly, uncertain what to do or say, "that 'twas against the law for us to couple."

Cam tried his best to calm her fears but didn't waiver in his resolve to gaze upon her, to hold her. He had dreamed of this for so long and he needed the contact. "We shan't couple." He held out a hand. "Just touch each other whilst I instruct you in your duties."

She thought that over for a moment, hesitant yet curious.

"Come," he said softly, "you belong to me now."

Kara bit down on her lip as she considered whether or not she should flee his rooms or comply. There had been many a time when the *Kefas* had massaged her into climax where she had wondered what 'twould feel like to have a warrior touch her thusly. Now she had the chance to find out. But should she take it, not yet knowing whether or not she had a care for him? Should she take it, when already she and Jana were secretly plotting to flee Tryston with Dari? Did she want to form a bond with the very man she planned to run from at first opportunity?

But Cam was right. She did belong to him. And refusing her charms to him would bring naught but suspicion down upon her head. Her mind made up to play it safe, she slowly removed first the top and then the bottom of the *mazi*. The sound of Cam sucking in his breath as his eyes raked over the black curls at her mons made her nipples plump up, which he also noticed.

"You are sweet perfection, Kara," he informed her as she accepted his large hand and came down on the bench to snuggle into his lap. Cam groaned as he ran one palm over her honey-gold breasts. Her nipples were but a scant inch from his mouth, their length as bedeviling as their thickness. "Hold my cock in your tiny hand," he murmured, "and stroke up and down the length of it."

She was curious despite her best attempts not to be, having many times wondered what a warrior's man-part would feel like. Clutching his warm cock firmly at the root with both hands, she slowly stroked up and down his shaft, enjoying the sounds of his breath catching in the back of his throat then growing increasingly labored. 'Twas a heady sort of power she wielded over him.

"Do you feel what you do to me?" he said thickly, his fingertips brushing through her hair. "Do you feel how hard I am for need of you?"

"Aye," she whispered. She continued to stroke him with one of her hands, her fingers running up and down his flesh, traveling over the prominent vein and up to the swollen head. Her other hand explored in the opposite direction, her fingers running through the golden curls at the root, then massaging his tight man sac.

"Mmm, Kara," he murmured, his fingers running through the dark locks cascading from her head, then down lower to brush her nipples, then lower still to splay through the black curls at the juncture of her thighs, "'tis bliss, your hands."

Kara's eyes closed on a soft moan when the pads of Cam's thumbs found her nipples and began to massage them in an agonizingly slow circular motion.

"Do you like that, wee one?"

"A-Aye."

"Would you like me to suckle from them?"

"Oh aye."

Cam secreted away a smile, thinking to himself that the course of action he'd decided on to confuse her reservation toward him would eventually, given enough of these sessions, bind her to him. She desired him physically, he knew.

Kara groaned as his mouth curled around one taut nipple, her head falling limp and her neck baring to him as he latched onto it and suckled from it. Her need was so pronounced that she released Cam's shaft without even realizing she had done so. "By the goddess," she breathed out, not having expected him to be as talented as her favored *Kefa*, "'tis more bliss than even my green slave provides."

The large fingers of one of his hands trailed between her legs, brushed through the black curls there, and found her clit. His man sac tightened and his shaft swelled when the sounds of her moans reached his ears. He suckled more harshly from the nipple she'd offered to him, the pad of his thumb massaging her erect woman's bud.

"*Oh aye,*" Kara groaned louder, her thighs automatically spreading wider to allow his hand better access to her channel. She reached out unthinkingly for his golden head and smashed it against her chest, needing him to suckle harder from her nipple. "*Please.*"

Cam complied, his teeth mentally gritting together from the torture of holding her, of bringing her toward peak, but of not being able to plunge deep inside of her. Seven Yessat years was a long time — too damned long.

Kara's eyes flew open on a groan of ecstasy, her nipple jutting out into Cam's suckling mouth, blood rushing to her face, as the most exquisitely ferocious orgasm she'd ever experienced tore through her belly with an intensity unknown to her until this moment. "*Cam.*"

The sound of her own voice calling out in passion to the very warrior whose lusty intentions she had been determined to thwart snapped her back into reality. Her glowing blue eyes rounded, her breathing choppy, she bolted up off of his lap and stared down at him in confusion.

She didn't know what to think, didn't know how to feel. The only thing she knew for a certainty was that her betrothed made her long for things she could never have if she were to flee Tryston with Jana and Dari.

When his golden head slowly came up and his piercing turquoise-green eyes found hers, Kara sucked in her breath. She felt a connectedness toward him, an unsettling empathy that induced her to feel guilt over planning to leave him.

Confused, her breathing still ragged, she turned from him and fled his rooms.

Cam stared after her, letting her go — for now. His lips kicked up into a semi-grin as he watched her naked golden buttocks make a beeline for the doors. He had rattled wee

Kara so badly that she had forgotten to put her *mazi* back on.

Arrogantly contented, Cam summoned her *mazi* back on for her as she fled, then summoned open the heavy doors to his apartments so she could run through them unimpeded. That accomplished, he summoned himself a bottle of *matpow* and settled down upon the *vesha* bench to drink from it.

He sighed heavily. 'Twas going to be a hellishly long seven Yessat years.

Chapter 17

Bloody hell! I'm going to kill him!

Giselle's eyes narrowed dangerously at her giddily smiling Sacred Mate as another puddle of oozing blue liquid came pouring out of her insides like—well she had no idea what it was like. Nothing, she thought grimly, could quite compare.

When a mammoth-sized oval structure began working its way out of her belly and into the world via her extremely small vagina, she thought she might swoon. "Oh my god!" she wailed dramatically, "It's going to tear me apart!"

Rem was too busy smiling from ear to ear to pay her drama much heed. "'Twould be considered a boon, my hearts, if you saw fit to hurry up a wee bit." His glowing blue eyes lit up as his hands spread out to catch the hatching *pani* sac like an empire at the World Series. "I am anxious to hold my little one."

Giselle's lips pinched together as she glowered up at him. Here she was giving birth to an egg on a hazy purple mountain like some wilderness hippie on a bad acid trip and all the man could think about was hurrying her up.

Bloody hell! As if she wasn't trying!

"Well excuuuuse me!" she said bitchily as she bore down and made another pushing attempt. "I didn't mean to inconvenience you!"

Rem ignored that. "'Tis almost here, my hearts." His forearms flexed as he steeled himself to catch it. "One more push and I'm a papa."

Giselle half laughed and half groaned. From Rem's rigid stance, one would think he was preparing to catch a catapulting freight train traveling at the speed of light.

With a final anguished groan and a last rush of oozing blue fluid, she bore down and pushed out the *pani* sac the rest of the way. Smiling once it was over, she watched through happy eyes as her husband clutched the incubating embryo to his chest, his hands shaking with emotion.

"One hour," he whispered reverently, "and we will know whether the goddess has given us a boy-child or a girl-child."

She felt his excitement and shared it as he came down on the rich purple soil and sat next to her. She ran her hand over the opaque embryo sac, completely in awe that she'd just hatched it. "Do you have a preference as to a boy or girl?" she asked softly.

"Nay." He shook his head as his gaze found hers and she noted with a pang of fierce love that tears had welled in his eyes. "I will be the happiest of papas either way."

Giselle craned her neck up to him, smiling when he bent his own head to kiss her. "I love you, Rem."

"I love you too, *nee'ka*."

And an hour later when the new parents discovered that the goddess had granted them both a boy-child and a girl-child, they both cried.

* * * * *

Rem awoke in the middle of the moon-rising to the feel of his life-force spurting into Giselle's mouth. His breathing ragged, he gritted his teeth as he ran his fingers through her silky strawberry-blonde hair. She was still drinking of him, suckling from the tiny hole at the crown of his cock to make certain she'd missed nothing. "You should have awoken me that I might have enjoyed more of your ministrations," he murmured, his voice still groggy with sleep.

"I couldn't wait," she said, planting tons of quick little kisses atop the head. "I needed to touch you, to hold you, to taste you..." Her face popped up into view and showed an impish grin. "...to thank you."

"For our *panis*?" he said softly. "'Tis I who thanks you, my hearts."

Giselle smiled, the mere mention of the twins that lay sleeping three feet away in the tent he had erected for their family enough to get her teary-eyed again. "Yes, I thank you for them," she whispered. She glanced toward their babies then back to her husband. "However," she admitted, "that wasn't why I felt compelled by the need to suck you off just now."

He raised a questioning eyebrow.

"Oh Rem," she breathed out, her smile tremulous, "thank you for *these*!"

Rem's jaw dropped open—in awe, disbelief, and desire—when he realized what it was he was being thanked for. Giselle's sweet juice had come in and as a result she now had *moosoos* the size of small planets. If the smile of bliss on her face and the way she kept rubbing her hands all about her breasts were any indication, then his wee *nee'ka* loved her fertile new form as much as he did.

"Do not," Rem ground out, his jaw clenching, "rub yourself like that in my presence until a fortnight is up." His glowing blue eyes narrowed in desire as he hungrily raked her form. Flipping her onto her back, he settled himself between her thighs to taste of her. "*Nee'ka*," he said hoarsely, "I will like as not die before a fortnight passes."

Giselle giggled. "They are wondrous breasts, are they not?" It seemed too much to hope for for a woman who'd been small-chested all of her life. "I think I'll write a poem about them," she teased.

He grinned. "We shall call it *Ode To The Moosoos*."

Her eyes lit up mischievously. "How about *Migi-Candy Mountains*?"

Rem's easy smile turned to rampant lust at the mere reminder of her spots. His nostrils flared as his eyes made love to the bedeviling freckles splashed across the tops of her *moosoos*. "You always know what to say," he ground out, "to get me hot."

Chapter 18

"She's spotted like the goddess," a harsh, unfamiliar male voice murmured.

"Aye," Giselle heard her husband reply with an arrogant sniff as one of his large palms swept over her breasts, "'tis enough to make a warrior spill his life-force for a certainty."

Rem's hand left her when one of the babies made a cooing sound. "And look at my wee hatchling," he boasted, "already she has a spotted nose like her *mani*."

The unfamiliar voice softened a bit. "She's your image in every other way, but aye, her wee nose is definitely spotted." The voice went impossibly lower. "'Tis happy I am for you, brother."

Brother?

Pulling herself from the depths of sleep, Giselle's eyes slowly opened to a purple twilight on Joo. Rem had opened the front of the tent, allowing the early morning lavender mist to swirl inside. It was a beautiful fog, but one she'd just as well never see again after leaving this place.

The first thing she noticed was that her newly born daughter Zari—whom Rem had wanted to name as a tribute to his eldest brother as well as his favored nieces Zora and Dari—was being cradled in the arms of a stranger who was built as massively as her husband. This could only be his brother.

The second thing she noticed was that the two brothers looked absolutely nothing alike. Where her husband was golden-haired, the other was dark-headed.

Where her husband smiled and was vastly contented, the other looked grim and troubled.

"Good morn, *nee'ka*," Rem said affectionately as she sat up on her elbows. "Give your greetings to my brother Kil."

Giselle smiled easily, too accustomed to being naked in front of Death and the other warriors these past two weeks to be embarrassed about her nudity or the fact that Kil's eyes were sweeping appreciatively over her body. Besides, now that she was built like a porn star she was more than happy to show it off.

Bloody hell! She loved having moosoos!

"It's a pleasure to meet you." She absently reached over and petted Bryony and Tess who were sound asleep beside her as she grinned up at the warlord her husband had described as ruthless. "Now I can finally put a face to one of the men we named our son after."

Kil's entire body stilled. His eyebrows shot up as he regarded Rem. "You named your heir for me?" he asked quietly.

"Aye." Rem smiled as he passed his son over to his brother. Now Kil held both babies. "For you and Dak."

"What's his name?" Kil asked as one side of his mouth kicked up into a semi-grin.

"Kilak," Giselle answered.

His gaze clashed with hers as he inclined his head. "You do me an honor."

"So," Rem asked as he took the babies from their uncle and bent to place them at Giselle's breasts, "you haven't yet said why it is you bothered to come here." One eyebrow rose fractionally. "And with your hunters no less."

Kil sighed. "Mayhap we should discuss this..." He glanced quickly toward Giselle then back to his brother. "...alone."

Her eyes narrowed. She didn't like to be kept in the dark. And worse yet, some strange premonition was whispering to her that he'd come here expecting trouble. "What is it?" she murmured as Rem settled the babies at her nipples. "I want to know too."

"Go on, brother," Rem said seriously. "Gis and I have been through too much together in so short a time. We've no secrets from the other."

Kil appeared to think that over. Eventually he relented on a sigh. "Let me come straight to the point then, brother. I came here with my hunters because I expect that we will be hunted." At Rem's furrowed brow, Kil gave him the truth in whole realizing it would serve naught to lie to him. He told him about the devolved creature, about its escape from the penal colony of Trukk, and about how the warrior guardsmen had died.

"So you see," he finished up by saying, "I feared for your safety. 'Tis common knowledge that predators do not exist on Joo, leastways no predators I've heard tell of." He shrugged his shoulders dismissively, but Giselle realized the gesture wasn't as casual as he'd intended it to be. They'd never say the words aloud, she knew, but these two brothers loved each other. "'Twould be passing easy to be ambushed unawares on a planet where the fiercest known animal is the *jee-jee* bug."

Rem had to grin at that. Giselle, however, was growing more upset by the second. She had a feeling that...oh god. "Kil?"

"Aye?"

"This...creature..." Her tongue darted out to wet her parched lips. "Is it? Is it...?" She sighed, her worried eyes meeting his.

"Aye," Kil said softly.

Rem took a deep breath. "'Twas what I almost became," he admitted aloud, surprising Kil.

"I didn't realize you had knowledge of your...devolution." His head cocked as he studied his brother's visage. "The Chief Priestess assures me that the joining did much to cure you." He pinned Giselle with his gaze. "If you have a care for my brother you will do as the most revered mystic amongst us advises and milk his rod as often as 'tis possible."

Giselle felt her cheeks pinken at his bluntness. "Of course."

Kil nodded, pleased by her quick reply.

"What else did Ari say?" Rem asked, wanting to know the whole of it.

Kil found his first smile as he clapped his brother on the back. "If your *nee'ka* milks your rod often then you will be completely cured in a few short Yessat years."

Giselle shook her head and sighed. She should have known the cure would be a sexual one. She shifted her gaze to the babies at her breasts.

Rem let out a breath of relief. "Thank the goddess."

"Aye." Kil nodded. "Oh—she also advises you to steer Giselle clear of consummation feasts until the predator has been totally submerged."

Rem's jaw clenched. "I agree," he ground out, the idea of her being touched by another warrior too unsettling to contemplate, "and 'tis one of the reasons I joined my *nee'ka* to me without—"

The sound of discharging *zykifs* outside of the tent brought Rem and Kil to immediate attention.

"What is it?" Giselle asked worriedly, her green eyes rounding with trepidation as her head shot up. "Why are they firing?"

Death's face appeared in the tent a moment later. He looked over to the two Kings as he bade Yoli with a gesture to go inside. "It's out there," he rumbled, his face uncharacteristically blanched. "And it's already killed two of your hunters, my friend."

Kil's nostrils flared. "By the sands!" he swore. Readying his weapon, he inclined his head to Rem. "'Tis best if you remain behind to guard the wenches and *panis.*"

Rem was already taking up a position by the door, his weapon prepared to detonate. "Aye," he agreed. "I will seal the tent when you take your leave." He hesitated for a brief moment. "But be careful, aye?"

Kil realized his brother thought him too battle-hungry as it was. Unfortunately, he conceded, 'twas naught but the truth. "Aye," he said softly.

And then he was gone, Death fast on his heels.

Wide-eyed, Giselle clutched the babies a bit tighter. She was quiet for a moment, but could only stand the suspense for so long. She needed a question answered.

After exchanging a worried look with Yoli, Giselle glanced toward Rem. "Is a devolved creature that powerful?" she whispered to her husband's back.

He stilled. She saw his muscles clench. "Aye," he murmured.

* * * * *

Rem kissed his wee hatchlings atop their fluffy golden heads, then bent his neck to sip from his *nee'ka's* lips. "Do not look so troubled, my love. I know in my hearts that

Death and my brother need me. But I *will* come back to you."

Giselle closed her eyes briefly as she dragged in a breath. "But what if the creature comes here and hurts the babies while—"

"Nay." Rem shook his head. "When I seal the tent, 'tis impossible for anything—*anything*—to break the shield."

She didn't like this, not one little bit. But neither would she try to keep him from doing what he felt was right. Giselle knew that if anything happened to Kil and Death when Rem could have aided them...

She sighed. He would never forgive himself.

"Gis," he said gently, nudging her chin up to force her to meet his gaze, "I will be back the soonest. 'Tis a vow amongst Sacred Mates."

She forced a smile to her lips. "I love you."

"And I love you." He kissed the tip of her spotted nose. "They've been gone for nigh unto two hours. I best leave."

As she watched him go, as she listened to the laser-like sound the tent emitted as it sealed, Giselle knew that Rem hadn't told her the entire truth. It wasn't just a worry for Kil and Death that had caused him to go.

He had also left for the creature. Rem didn't want any warrior save himself to extinguish the life of that which he'd almost become.

Chapter 19

For an hour Rem tracked the creature through the carnage it had left behind. Mangled, bloody body parts were scattered every few minutes or so, a testament to the creature's brute strength that it could make short work of at least five armed hunters.

But then, as if it had disappeared into thin air, the trail of dined upon carcasses stopped abruptly. For another solid hour Rem continued to track it, further and further into the silvered jungles of Mount Lia until he at last realized he was being led in a loop of sorts.

Coming to an abrupt halt, he breathed in deeply and allowed something to happen that he knew was dangerous to arouse. He invited the predator in him to surface. 'Twas mayhap foolhardy, but he sensed that his brother and best friend's lives might hinge upon it.

His eyes flicking a warning green, his teeth baring slightly, Rem invited enough of the predator to emerge that his senses might be tripled in their intensity. He smiled without humor when, a moment later, he detected three scents that under normal circumstances he would not have been able to track unless the scent had belonged to his Sacred Mate.

All three scents were male, he noted, but only two were familiar. Allowing the predator to emerge a bit more, his head shot up and he darted his glowing green gaze in the appropriate direction. The scents were headed south. Toward Giselle and his hatchlings.

Fangs exploded into his mouth fully, the challenge to his territory and possessions not allowed to go unpunished even though 'twas impossible to break the tent's seal should the creature find them. As his body darted through the silvered trees with unnatural speed, his senses following the scent of warm blood and beating hearts, it occurred to Rem from somewhere in the haze of his mind that only a small part of who he was remained. The rest was all predator.

* * * * *

Giselle and Yoli huddled together with the *panis* and dogs and screamed while the creature made yet another attempt to slice through the tent. The sound of its razor-sharp nails scraping against the sealed structure was terrifying in the extreme.

The women had tried to remain quiet at first, hoping it would give up and go away after meeting with a lack of success. But after several minutes had passed by and it began to sound as though the creature was making some headway into getting through the seal, they had both started screaming in the hopes that Rem would hear their cries from wherever he was and come save them.

The clawing stopped altogether, inducing the women to cease their yelling and dart their eyes about the tent nervously. Her breathing ragged, Giselle closed her eyes and silently cried when she realized the new sound she heard was a sniffing one. The creature was running its nose about the fortress, making certain its prey was still inside. Satisfied that it was, it began to claw at the tent's material again.

Giselle could withstand no more. If they were all slated to die this day then she wanted to be prepared for whatever it was that meant to take them out. She needed to see this thing, didn't want any heart-stopping last minute surprises as the creature clawed its way through the structure and snuffed out their lives.

Handing Kilak over to Yoli who was already cradling Zari, Giselle slowly crawled to the front of the tent, preparing not to open it, but to peep through the portal that permitted one to see outside. Her entire body was shaking as she fixed her eye against the portal peep and, dragging in a ragged breath, scanned the perimeter for the creature.

There it was.

Giselle sucked in her breath at the hideous sight that greeted her. This creature, this...thing, was a gross caricature of its former self. Its naked body was gigantic and as thickly muscled as any warrior's, but was also possessed of a metallic blue skin that doubled as a shield of armor. Red, razor-sharp nails jutted out of each of its digits. Its face was hideously distorted, veins bulging at the temples as though they meant to pop through, serrated dagger-like teeth protruding from its mouth, still dripping of blood from a fresh kill.

But it was the eyes that got to her, the eyes that looked so much like Rem's during his bouts of near-madness. They were a dull glowing green with piercing rays of light flecks that brought to mind old reruns of the TV show *The Incredible Hulk* when mild-mannered Bruce Banner would snap and his eyes would light up as he prepared to transform into his other, baser self. Those eyes gave her the shivers.

Giselle bit down on her lip nervously when the creature moved from out of her sites. "Where did you go?" she murmured, pressing her eye closer to the porthole. "Where are—*oh Jesus.*"

One lit-up green eye appeared on the other side of the porthole, pressing itself against the crystal viewer to gaze back at her. Instinctively jumping away, she fell on her buttocks to the ground.

Her heart-rate picking up so rapidly she could feel blood rushing to her face, Giselle crawled back toward Yoli and her children in fast movements and huddled with them. She met the bound servant's gaze. "If it finds a way to break in," she whispered, "we'll never survive it."

Wide-eyed, Yoli nodded her understanding. "'Tis glad I am," she whispered back, "that I will not have to die alone."

Giselle closed her eyes briefly. "Me too," she murmured. She reached out and squeezed the bound servant's hand. "I don't know how you were captured or why, but for whatever it's worth I'm sorry your last moments might end in captivity."

Yoli squeezed her hand back. "I've less than a Yessat year's worth of servitude left, but it hasn't been so bad."

Giselle was curious about her despite the dire circumstances. Besides, if they were going to die, they might as well calm each other with talking rather than spend their last moments worrying about what would happen anyway. She picked Zari up and kissed the top of her head before turning her gaze back to Yoli. "If we were to survive and you returned to Death's sector with him, what would you do when he released you?"

"I'd stay with him if he'd have me, but 'tis well known that warriors grow bored with bedmates who are not *nee'kas* very quickly." She shrugged absently, her massive breasts jiggling a bit as she did so. "Leastways, I'll perchance have enough credits by then to make a better life for myself than I'd had before my capture."

"How so?"

"Bound servants are permitted to keep what their masters adorn them in when they are released. In truth, the quality of just one of the *qi'ka* skirts we wear is fine enough to be traded at market for many credits." She grinned. "Besides the promise of pleasure, 'tis the reason why you'll often times find that servants compete mightily for the master's attention. The more he covets you, the better he'll adorn you, dressing you up like a favored doll."

Giselle's lips pinched together in a frown. It was so deplorable to treat women as sexual chattel, but she knew none of the warriors saw it that way. They felt it was their right to take what they would.

She thought about the skirts that made up the bottom half of the *qi'ka* and could see the truth in what Yoli had said. What Giselle knew about otherworldly clothing material was next to nothing, but the way they shimmered brought to mind precious gems and she could only assume that somehow the material was spun with them.

A deafening thump on the top of the tent broke the women from their talking. Giselle sucked in her breath, staring up at the ceiling in horror when she realized that the creature was trying its luck up there. And if her ears hadn't deceived her, if what she had just heard was indeed a tiny tear in the seal, then the monster's luck had just turned for the better while theirs had just run out.

The women huddled closer together, the children between them. Bryony and Tess, sensing that they were being stalked by something that they could not get away from, made little whimpering sounds as they settled bodily against Giselle.

The women screamed as the tent seal popped and the creature burst through the roof, landing on its feet in front of them.

* * * * *

Rem followed the two familiar scents, bursting through the trunk of a silver tree to get to them. He was so relieved to find Kil and Death intact and uneaten that before he'd realized what had happened, the predator within him had submerged and he was fully a warrior once again.

His eyes flicked a final warning green before returning fully to blue and shutting off. Panting heavily from his earlier run, he squatted down over the two bodies and felt for hearts beats. He let out a breath of relief. They were both alive.

Kil was the first to emerge from unconsciousness, rubbing his temples as he slowly sat up. "By the sands," he grumbled, accepting a hands up from Rem then turning around to offer the same to Death, "never let it get out you found me thusly, brother."

Rem found his first smile in many hours. "'Tis strange indeed to find the mighty warlord Kil Q'an Tal in the after-effects of a swoon."

Kil's eyes narrowed dangerously. "I did not swoon," he gritted out.

Rem merely chuckled.

Realizing he was being teased, he let his brother's insolent remark go by and threw a hand toward a mangled carcass a ways back. "It struck without warning. We had no time to discharge our weapons, not even a moment to use our powers." He shook his head. "The creature burst through the trees with such a show of force that I suspect 'twas the catapulting trees themselves that knocked Death and I out."

Death nodded. "Aye," he grumbled. "I saw them shower toward us a fraction of a Nuba-second before we were sprayed with them."

Rem glanced over at the thick, heavy trees that were topped off with sharp branches. They were lucky they had been merely knocked out and not impaled by some of the sharper fronds. He glanced back to the carcass, his eyes closing briefly when it dawned on him 'twas one of his own men lying over there half-eaten. "How many are dead?"

"Before we were knocked out about nine," Kil answered, brushing off the back of his leathers. "I've no idea how long we were unconscious so now 'tis hard to say."

"I wonder," Rem said as his forehead wrinkled, "why the creature didn't bother taking the deuce of you out whilst you were knocked out unawares."

Kil and Death had no answer to that. "'Tis hard to say. Mayhap it prefers tracking moving prey."

"For the thrill," Death agreed in his baritone rumble.

"Where were the remaining hunters," Rem asked, "when last you knew?"

"I had them spread out to all areas of the mountain to hunt." Kil shook his head. "They could be anywhere do they live."

"Is there a rendezvous time?"

"Aye. In approximately three more hours."

Rem nodded. "We'll have a better idea of the death toll in three hours time then."

Kil let out a breath, feeling as though he'd led his own men into a death trap. "Aye," he agreed in a murmur.

The sounds of female screaming reached all three warriors' ears simultaneously. Rem's eyes widened and his hearts rate picked up. "*Nee'ka*," he said softly. With one last burst of unnatural speed, he set off through the forest.

Chapter 20

Giselle and Yoli scooted away from the devolved beast, a reflexive action destined to serve no purpose. The remainder of the tent had been scattered to the purple winds, leaving them completely bared to the elements. The primal instinct to stay alive, to protect her children, took over and Giselle's eyes began darting about seeking a method of escape.

There was nothing. Behind them there was a steep cliff, its sharp drop to the valley below tantalizing them with a lure of instant death. In front of them there was the creature, its massive dagger-like teeth protruding from its mouth in preparation of feasting. The women glanced toward each other, deciding in that moment it would be best to plummet over the cliff. They scooted closer to the edge.

The creature, sensing it was about to lose its prey, leapt closer, its massive legs lunging with a frightening speed toward them. The women screamed, realizing they had made their decision to jump a second too late.

Wide-eyed and breathing raggedly, Giselle whimpered as the beast closed in. Handing over Zari to Yoli, she shielded them all behind her in an instinctive gesture. She knew she was about to die, saw it in the beasts' eyes. "Run!" she said frantically to Yoli. "At least try to run!"

Yoli did as she'd been bade, clutching the hatchlings to her breasts as she made a beeline for the jungle. The creature tracked their movement with its lit-up eyes and hesitated. Knowing it was deciding whether or not to follow them, Giselle snagged its attention back to her.

"Just take me!" she screamed, unable to bear the thought of what would become of Rem if their babies didn't live and equally unable to bear the thought of her children dying so heinously. "I'm here you bastard right in front of your face! Just take me!"

The creature decided on expedience, his head darting back to size her up. Whipping out its massive arms, Giselle was plucked up off of the ground in less time than it took to blink. Its razor-sharp nails dug into her skin and induced droplets of blood to flow down her arms as it drew her in closer to its mouth.

She closed her eyes tightly, unable to watch. Her breathing labored, it took her a suspended moment to realize that nothing was happening. No teeth had cut into her. No fangs had ripped open her neck. Unable to bear the suspense a moment longer, her eyes flew open to see why the creature had paused.

It was staring at her. No, not at her precisely, but at her...freckles.

The creature released her and she plummeted to the ground, the impact of the fall jarring her knees. She was so dumbstruck at what was happening before her that all she could do was scramble to her feet and watch, the thought to run never once dawning on her.

This devolved being, this creature, was fighting within itself. Just as Rem's eyes had flickered back and forth on past occasions so too was this monster's. Something about her had triggered some distant memory, some past recollection of a former life and a former self.

Giselle felt tears welling up in her eyes as she stared at this thing that had almost been her husband. Like Rem, this beast had once been a man with all the hopes and dreams for a happy future that any other man harbored. But somewhere along the line something had happened and his mind had snapped. Biology had taken over from there, devolving him into the Trystonni version of the missing link.

The creature's eyes flicked back and forth in color, in the end remaining their lit-up green. Where Rem had been able to defend himself against the changes, this being was too far gone. And worse yet, he knew it.

Giselle pressed a hand to her mouth the moment she understood what the creature meant to do. In a piercing and no doubt short-lived moment of sanity, it looked down at her and whispered "forgive me Aparna" before throwing itself off of the cliff.

She walked the few steps it took to bring her to the cliff's edge and watched the creature plummet for long moments before finding death by impalement on the sharp branch of a silver tree in the valley below.

Giselle sank to her knees and took a deep breath. "Bloody hell," she murmured.

* * * * *

Rem found his *nee'ka* sitting by the cliff, staring unblinkingly at the remains of the devolved creature below. She didn't move when he placed a hand on her shoulder and he suspected he knew the reason why. He had failed her. She wanted him no more.

"Giselle," he said softly, cradling her from behind, "when I left to find my brother and Death I truly believed 'twas impossible to break that seal." He ran his hands over her breasts from behind, just needing to feel her, to be close to her. "I know 'twill take many, many moon-risings, my hearts, but I can only pray you will come to forgive me."

154

"Rem—"

"'Tis for a certainty," he interrupted her, his voice rough with emotion, "that I deserve no forgiveness. I should never have left you," he whispered fiercely, "not ever." He squeezed her tighter. "But I can vow this very moment 'twill not happen again."

"Rem—"

"By the goddess," he ground out, the veins in his biceps bulging as he held her, "'twould have driven me to my devolution had you died."

She cocked her head to glance at him from over her shoulder. "May I speak now?" she asked with a teasing smile.

He eyed her warily. "That depends upon your verdict."

Her nose crinkled. "Verdict?"

"On whether or not you will forgive me."

She sighed. "You take the alpha male thing to appalling extremes at times." At his furrowed brow she clarified that statement a bit. "Don't be an idiot, there's nothing to forgive."

He ran his hands over her breasts and groaned. "Ah *nee'ka*, I would that I could believe that."

"It's true. I can't fault you for doing the right thing." Her nod was definitive. "You thought you could help Kil and Death and you thought the seal was impenetrable. You made the best decision based upon what you knew at the time."

"Ah, wee one, you are too good to me."

She smiled as she snuggled back into his large frame, enjoying the feel of his warm hands massaging her engorged breasts. They were quiet for a long moment, both of them content to hold the other without speaking. Eventually it was Rem who broke the silence.

"How?" he said simply.

She knew what he meant without questioning him. "He thought I was the goddess you worship."

Rem's hands stilled on her breasts. "The spots?"

"Uh huh."

He resumed the massage. "I told you true when I said they were bedeviling."

She closed her eyes and smiled when the massage reached her nipples. She didn't want to think of the creature any longer. It was dead. It would cause no more pain and it would be in no more pain. "How long until a fortnight?" she murmured, changing the subject.

He sighed wearily. "Twelve Yessat days, thirty Nuba-hours, and seventeen Nuba-minutes."

"Bloody hell."

Chapter 21

Twelve days later on Sypar...

Giselle's lips pinched together in a frown as she walked through the wintry fresh gardens of the Ice Palace with her new sisters-in-law. She shook her head and sighed as the group stumbled upon the High King Jor, his eyes closed in bliss as his harem attended to his needs right there in the middle of her ice-gardens.

Naked bound servants were all over the massive warrior, massaging his chest, popping plump nipples into his mouth, riding his cock into bliss.

"I hate to ask you this," Giselle said to Kyra and Geris, "but do I have this to look forward to with Kilak as well?"

Kyra sighed like a martyr. "Uh huh." She glanced down at her coupling son and shook her head in defeat. "Truth be told it doesn't bother me any longer. I mean, at least he comes out and does it where I can see him now."

Giselle gawked at her. "You *want* to see it?"

Geris chuckled. "That's not what she meant." She shook her head and grinned. "I remember when my son Dar turned thirteen and got his harem. I didn't see heads or tails from my boy for a solid three weeks. He stayed in his rooms and played with his bound servants day and night."

Giselle laughed. "I take your point. In other words," she said to Kyra, "you put up with the sight of him coupling just so you can see him."

The Empress glanced down at her son during the same moment he spurted his life-force into the channel of his favored bound servant. Her lips pinched together. "Yep. That about covers it."

Giselle half snorted and half laughed as the trio turned on their heels and made their way back to the great hall. It was amazing, simply astounding, that her life had been altered so fundamentally within so short of a time period. But all for the better. Definitely all for the better.

"This palace is gorgeous," Geris remarked as they strode toward where their warriors and children were sitting around the raised table talking, drinking *matpow*, eating, and laughing. Since Giselle couldn't have a consummation feast the family had decided to throw a celebratory feast on her behalf instead. "When Dak told me it was called the Ice Palace I had no idea he'd meant it literally."

Giselle nodded, warming to the topic. She loved it here as well, though they'd only been home a few short days. "The atmosphere of the entire moon is rather on the frosty side and, indeed, the palace itself was molded from ice-jewels."

Kyra's brow wrinkled. "Ice-jewels?"

"Yes." She pointed towards an ice-jeweled wall. "In the deepest ice-mines of Sypar, splinters of ice fuse with precious white gems to create the ice-jewel. The process takes thousands of Yessat years to accomplish which is why the gem is so costly."

"That is so cool." Kyra grinned. "I didn't even know such a thing existed. But then again, Rem was never much of a talker. Not until he found you that is."

Giselle smiled. "I really love him."

"I know. And he really loves you. I'm glad you two found each other."

When Giselle's eyes clashed with Rem's as she strode toward him, she told herself again how lucky she was. Never in all of her wildest dreams from the sleepy little country town of Shoreham had she ever expected to find such vast contentment.

Settling herself next to her Sacred Mate who was busily showing off their *panis* to his brothers, Giselle ran a hand over his strong jaw then cuddled against him as she listened to the conversation taking place.

"I apologize brothers," Kil said as he raised his goblet of *matpow* to his lips, "but I fear I must leave this moon-rising to see to my sectors."

Zor raised an eyebrow. "You've been seeing to your sectors a lot as of late. I hope there is naught amiss?"

Ah, but there is plenty amiss. Your foolish brother cannot stand to be separated from his own bedeviling bound servant. "Nay," Kil murmured, "naught is amiss."

Giselle glanced up at Rem and grinned when she felt him place a kiss on the tip of her spotted nose. "You know what tonight is, don't you?" she whispered.

His eyes raked over her hungrily, settling over-long at her engorged breasts. Her *moosoos*, he noted, looked resplendid this moon-rising in the shimmering black *qi'ka* she wore. "Think you I can forget, wench?" He bent his neck to place tantalizing kisses behind her ear and on her neck. "Take my hatchlings upstairs, *nee'ka*, and have them put abed," he said thickly. "I shall make our excuses and follow right behind."

"Mmm," she whispered, the flesh between her thighs already wetting for him, "will do." Standing up, she winked across the table to Kyra and Geris who grinned back at her then took Zari and Kilak from her husband's massive arms. She kissed their fluffy golden heads, inhaling their fresh baby scents.

Rem threw her a worried look. "'Tis too much weight, Gis. Give me one of my hatchlings and I'll go up with you anon."

So they both made their excuses to their family before rushing upstairs to put their hatchlings down for the night. "I've a surprise for you when at last we're alone," Rem murmured as they finally reached the second floor.

She grinned. "I can hardly wait to see it."

Five minutes later when they were alone in their bedchamber and Rem summoned off her *qi'ka*, Giselle began to laugh hysterically when her husband held up his present.

He grinned back, a charming dimple popping out. "I had it specially made for you, my hearts. It cost over five thousand credits I'll have you know."

She shook her head and chuckled. "An ice-jewel papoose?"

His eyebrows waggled. "Aye. And 'tis *vesha* soft," he said through glazed-over eyes.

Giselle sucked in her breath as he harnessed her, plucking her off of the ground, slipping her through the papoose, and impaling her all in one fluid motion. "Oh Rem," she breathed out, "I've missed your cock so much."

"Have you?" he ground out, his jaw clenching as he began to walk about the bedchamber.

"Oh yes."

"Shall I walk faster for you then, my lusty little wench?"

"Oh Rem — *oh yes.*"

He bounced her up and down on his shaft, the sound of her greedy moans like music to his ears. Her engorged breasts jiggled wantonly, inducing him to palm the heavy globes and suckle from them.

"Faster. Walk faster."

"Mmm," he murmured in between laps at her nipples, "'tis a good *nee'ka* who begs for her Sacred Mate's cock." He walked faster, the popping sound of a nipple leaving his mouth echoing in the bedchamber as he gritted his teeth at her tight flesh. "How does this feel?" he asked arrogantly, impaling her channel mercilessly.

Giselle groaned. Licking her lips seductively, she met his gaze as she ran her fingers about her spots. "It's making them tingle," she whispered.

Rem's nostrils flared as he clutched her hips and prepared to spurt his life-force deep in her channel. "Then this should make them scream, my little papoose-wearing seductress."

As her bridal necklace began to pulse, Giselle could only agree.

Bloody hell! She loved her papoose!

Epilogue
The dominant red moon of Morak,
later that moon-rising...

She was gone. She had run away.

Bellowing like a madman, Kil's fist came crashing down upon the closest tabletop, shattering the crystal structure into a million pieces.

She had left him. She had dared to escape him whilst he'd been away.

Barking at one of his warriors to prepare a highspeed conveyance for his departure, Kil's heavy footfalls could be heard throughout the palace corridor as he made his way to the launching pad.

If she thought she could escape him, he told himself grimly, then she had better think again. He would find her. He had a lock on her scent.

The scar on his cheek twisted in rage as he alighted into his high-speed conveyance. In the midst of his fury it never dawned on the King of Morak that there was a reason he was able to get a lock on her scent to begin with. All he knew was that he had to have her back. And he had to have her anon.

King Kil Q'an Tal, the most feared and ruthless warlord that the time dimensions had ever known, launched from the conveyance pad preparing to do what it was he did best. He was preparing to hunt. The only difference, he thought as his jaw clenched unforgivingly, was that this time what he hunted was a wench.

* * * * *

She accepted the bag of credits from the tradesman who had offered her a high price for one of her *qi'kas*. Glancing over her shoulder to make certain she wasn't being followed, she fled into the busy village and made her way towards the tiny crystal shack she was hiding out in.

She stopped for a moment as a strange flutter quivered through her belly. That was the second time in as many weeks. Reminding herself that she had no time to ponder the foreign sensation, she walked briskly into the village centre, her scent mingling as one with the other passersby.

* * * * *

Next in the Trek Mi Q'an Series:

ENSLAVED

ISBN # 0-9724377-7-0

His glowing blue eyes summoned the primitive weapon from her grasp. Shuddering with fear, she realized she had just lost the only thing standing between her freedom and becoming... *Enslaved*.

About the author:

Critically acclaimed and highly prolific, Jaid Black is the best-selling author of numerous erotic romance tales. Her first title, *The Empress' New Clothes*, was recognized as a readers' favorite in women's erotica by Romantic Times magazine. A full-time writer, Jaid lives in a cozy little village in the northeastern United States with her two children. In her spare time, she enjoys traveling, horseback riding, and furthering her collection of African and Egyptian art.

She welcomes mail from readers. You can visit her on the web at www.jaidblack.com or write to her c/o Ellora's Cave Publishing at P.O. Box 787, Hudson, Ohio 44236-0787.

COMING SOON:

Three reigning queens of erotic romance. Three titillating tales of
lust and love set in future worlds. One highly anticipated book…

VENUS IS BURNING

ISBN # 0-9724377-5-4

A futuristic erotic romance anthology

Devilish Dot by Jaid Black
Hot To The Touch by Marly Chance
Road To Rapture by Marilyn Lee

COMING SOON:

ENCHAINED

An erotic bondage romance anthology

**Death Row: The Mastering by Jaid Black
Mastered by Ann Jacobs
A Choice Of Masters by Joey W. Hill**

COMING SOON:

THE PORTAL

An erotic time travel romance anthology

Warlord by Jaid Black (medieval Scotland)
The Seduction Of Sean Nolan by Treva Harte (Civil War)
Tears Of Amun by Jordan Summers (ancient Egypt)

Printed in the United States
22631LVS00006B/133-162